Later that night, the siren positioned on a pole directly across from Jessie and Lynn's bedroom went off. Jessie jerked awake and Lynn reached over to calm her. "You're okay. It's just that goofy siren across the street. I can't believe in this day and age with beepers, they use this outdated system to call their emergency crews. I wonder what's going on."

The flashing lights shown into the bedroom as they went by, and Jessie got out of bed and peered out.

"They're going around the corner past Chris and Pam's house. That's the street the stairs up the hill are on. Probably some drunken student had an accident."

"I wouldn't be surprised, since that's the drug of choice for these kids," Lynn replied. "Come back to bed."

About the Author

Annette Van Dyke teaches women's studies at a state university in the Midwest where she lives with her life partner of twenty-plus years and their five cats. This is her first mystery novel, but she regularly publishes in the field of lesbian studies.

A JESSIE BATELLE MYSTERY

HOODED murder

Annette Van Dyke

THE NAIAD PRESS, INC.
1996

Printed in the United States of America on acid-free paper
First Edition

Editor: Christine Cassidy
Cover designer: Bonnie Liss (Phoenix Graphics)
Typesetter: Sandi Stancil

Library of Congress Cataloging-in-Publication Data

Van Dyke, Annette Joy.
  Hooded murder / by Annette Van Dyke.
    p.   cm.
  ISBN 1-56280-134-1 (pbk. : alk. paper)
  1. Women detectives—United States—Fiction. 2.
Lesbians—United States—Fiction. I. Title.
PS3572.A4298H66   1996
813'.54—dc20   95-51024
                                                      CIP

*For Susan and Kathy
and my Friday night writing group:
Martha, Sandy, Jennifer, and Cheryl*

CHAPTER 1

Jessie Batelle gathered up her papers and books and dropped them into her briefcase, peering into the tiny mirror someone had pasted under the bookshelf over her desk. She ran a comb through her unruly brown hair and sighed at the latest gray hairs. She'd just been hired at Burford College and this was the first all-faculty meeting of the fall semester. She was already late for the new faculty introductions which started a half-hour before her class ended. She nervously picked up her briefcase, pulling the door to her office shut, and hurried down the now empty hall

1

out of the building. She crossed the grassy quad that was surrounded by massive brick buildings and headed to the auditorium housed in the 1960s-style student union. It had probably been an offering by the administration to quiet any student unrest at being treated as children. Jessie was surprised by the students of Burford. Most were from wealthy homes. She wondered why they would choose Burford, a second-tier school in the world of expensive private liberal arts schools, a place she'd never heard of before reading the employment ads in the *Chronicle of Higher Education*.

Situated at the top of a hill overlooking the tiny Victorian village, Burford was a small campus tucked away in the Midwest. A drive circled the campus, coming up from the one block of stores and village businesses that constituted Main Street and coming down the other side past the athletic field. The only other way off the hill was some steps cut into the hillside that went from the student housing to the village houses below. Jessie understood that parents would see the isolation of Burford as a means of keeping their kids out of trouble, but rumor had it that the students stirred up their own trouble.

In recent years, an all-male prankster group had focused on harassing women, gays and lesbians on campus, using ugly, pornographic flyers. The student social life on the campus was controlled by the fraternity men — unlike other campuses on which the Greek influence had waned. Acquaintance rape, not even date rape, was common. The latest fad at fraternity parties was to serve Jello cubes made with vodka to an unsuspecting freshwoman who would quickly ingest more alcohol than she could handle.

From there, she would wake up in some guy's bed without remembering how she got there. If she had been a virgin before, she was a virgin no longer.

Jessie pulled the heavy glass door open, climbed the stairs and waited for the elevator. The wall clock said she was only a little late. When she finally stepped from the elevator, Jessie saw that the auditorium doors were still open. It looked as if they were just starting. Jessie stood in the doorway for a minute, looking for a seat. Chris Stendal, who directed the Women's Center and had the office next to hers, spotted Jessie and pointed to the seat beside her. Jessie walked quickly down the aisle into Chris's row, pushed her briefcase under the seat and sat down.

Chris whispered, "I was wondering what happened to you. I'm supposed to introduce you."

Jessie adjusted her skirt, a concession to the occasion, as she whispered back, "My class goes until four-thirty. I had to let them out early to be here."

Jessie watched as each new faculty member was introduced by someone in her or his department. There were a surprising number of new faculty — quite a few women in the math area. She was the untenured chair of a small interdisciplinary women's studies program, and Chris Stendal had been tapped to introduce her. When it was her turn, Chris, who had apparently been fishing for something which would give some personal note to the introduction said, "I'm known for my dogs and I was going to introduce Jessie as a cat person since she has three cats, but instead she should be introduced as the plant woman. She has brought dozens of plants with her and has already put out planter boxes under the

3

windows of her faculty house at the bottom of the hill."

Jessie couldn't decide how she felt about the comments. They seemed a little odd but were, she supposed, unoffensive. When the introductions were over, Jessie and Chris got up to leave. "Are you bringing your partner Pam to the reception?" Jessie asked.

"Pam usually comes, but today she's not feeling well. You're bringing Lynn to the reception, aren't you? You really should. I know the students are conservative, but the president makes a real effort to be inclusive." Chris gathered up her purple bookbag.

"I'm picking her up at the house. I'll see you there."

"Oh, I should warn you about Joyce. We call her the lesbian vampire."

So many new people, Jessie thought. "Have I met her?"

"Probably not, but she'll be at the reception. She can be charming. She's good at attracting new faculty when they're vulnerable, then dumping them and wrecking havoc. It happened to me when I came here a few years ago. She's slept with almost every lesbian faculty on campus and even some students. Last year a student brought a sexual harassment charge against her. Stay clear of her," Chris said ominously.

Jessie wondered where Chris's partner Pam Effelton was when all this was going on.

She must have looked skeptical because Chris shrugged almost apologetically and said, "I moved out here by myself. Pam and I were at odds. I guess I was lonely. It started innocently enough. Before I

4

knew it, I was going over to Joyce Barnette's at lunch and spending the night. Joyce's house is right across from Denise Oberon's — she was the chair of the search committee, remember?

Jessie nodded.

"Anyway, it wasn't long before everyone knew. Denise had been involved with her, too, you know, and also got hurt. When the student came to me because I run the program for sexual-assault victims, I thought we had her. We tried to get her fired."

"Really?"

"Don't ask me how she hung on. We did our best," Chris said as she walked out of the auditorium and down the sidewalk toward home. Just before she was out of earshot, Chris turned and yelled, "Oh, you and Lynn are coming to the party tonight, aren't you? It will be a chance to meet everyone."

"We wouldn't miss it. What should we bring?'

"Nothing, really. You're the guests of honor." Chris waved and went on.

Jessie felt uncomfortable about the investigation of the student charge against Joyce being carried out by an ex-lover. That seemed a little too incestuous even for a lesbian community, Denise had spread the word about Chris and Joyce, too, and then ganged up on Joyce after the break up, or did Denise have something to do with the break up? And then there was Chris's old lover, Pam. How was she going to keep all these animosities straight in her position as Director of Women's Studies? she wondered as she watched Chris disappear down the hill. Chris's information gave a Jessie sinking feeling as she thought of conducting amicable meetings with all of

5

these women. That they be one happy family was always a requirement of women's studies programs. What had she gotten herself into?

Later, at the reception on the president's lawn at the bottom of the hill, Jessie got a look at Joyce Barnette. She didn't appear too dangerous — she wasn't a flashy kind of person. A casual dresser, she had sandy-colored short hair, a nice smile and freckles. She didn't look like the femme fatale Jessie associated with "vampire." Jessie didn't have time to worry much about Joyce, however; she was more worried about her partner, Lynn Perry, whose blood pressure seemed to be acting up from the stress of the situation. Lynn, a rural, working-class lesbian, was not doing well making small talk with the faculty, many of whom had gotten their under-graduate degrees at Burford. Jessie heard Lynn's speech starting to slur, and she rushed to rescue her from the Dean.

"Dean Whippet, you've met Lynn? Nice reception, hmm? The food is especially nice. Someone told me that the food isn't as elaborate as in former years, but it's certainly more than I'm used to coming from a state university. Lynn, want to get some shrimp?" Jessie steered her over to one of the tables laden with food and drink. "Want to go home? You don't look like you feel well."

At the edge of the crowd, Joyce and Chris seemed to be having a very intense conversation. Chris had changed into a trendy, bright red suit with a very short skirt. Jessie heard Chris hiss, "I told you, stay away from her! I won't have this start again!"

Just then Lynn stumbled on the uneven ground.

Jessie grabbed her arm to steady her. They were out of range of Joyce and Chris's conversation.

As they walked alone down the tree-lined village street toward home, a woman in a denim vest and skirt approached.

"Who's that?" Lynn asked. "Do you know her? She seems to be staring at us."

Jessie squinted into the distance. "I can't see well without my glasses. Oh, that's Lucy Taft, the chair of the other department besides women's studies with which I'm supposed to be connected."

"We're having a party at my house next weekend for department members and friends and I want you and your partner — what's her name? — to feel welcome," Lucy said abruptly, as if Lynn wasn't standing there.

"Oh, thanks," Jessie said, watching her stride away in her long skirt and Birkenstocks.

She wondered why Lucy seemed so awkward in extending the invitation. Jessie wasn't sure she was going to like living in this fishbowl — a faculty house at the bottom of the campus hill, lesbian faculty who formed no kind of community in a hostile fraternity environment and a partner who already seemed to be crumbling under the pressure.

As they neared the house, Joyce Barnette rushed past them, heading up the hill, the back way to the campus on the somewhat treacherous steps built into the hillside. "She must be pretty angry to take those steep steps two at a time," Jessie remarked.

"She almost knocked me over," Lynn said.

They watched as Joyce disappeared onto campus.

"So far, Denise has been right about there being

no community," Jessie said, remembering the scene they had just witnessed between Chris and Joyce. "There seems to be so much conflict between the lesbian faculty. I wonder if the administration is as supportive as Chris says." Jessie remembered her interview for the women's studies position.

As chair of the search committee, Denise Oberon had hosted Jessie during her visit. On the half-hour drive from the airport, Jessie had tried to size her up. Probably in her early 40s, she was dressed casually, if a little preppy, in a sweater and pants under her wool coat. Jessie noticed her tiny post earrings and the way her light brown hair waved back behind her ears. Despite there being no obvious signs — no labyris, women's symbols or earcuff — Jessie guessed that she was a sister, but she'd been surprised by Denise's guarded manner when they visited Denise's home to walk her dog before dinner. Pushing away the slobbering spaniel, Jessie had been introduced to Denise's "housemate," Jennifer, a tall, dark-haired women a bit younger than Denise.

"Your 'housemate'?" Jessie had asked.

The situation had all the markings of a lesbian partnership, but Denise replied easily, "We just share a house, nothing more. I own the house."

They walked the dog around the quiet block and Jessie admired Denise's turn-of-the-century home. She asked, "What's it like for women to live in a small community that prides itself on its Victorian heritage?"

Denise laughed, her broad mouth in a lopsided grin and her short brown hair blowing in the crisp breeze. "You know, they say that the reason Burford women students can't live in their sorority houses is

8

because there was a law on the books in the eighteen hundreds that more than ten women living together in one house made the place a brothel."

"You're kidding! But what about now? Surely that law doesn't still exist?"

"Now it's custom and the houses are too small, so only the men live in their houses. The women all live in the residence halls. There isn't even any women's community at Burford, even though we have a lot of women faculty involved in women's studies."

Jessie thought that if she came to work there, she would try to change that. In fact, she considered bringing people together to be one of her strengths, but it would take time. After all, she was rewriting her dissertation on feminist communities in academia for publication. She was excited about the opportunity to be the tenure-tracked director of women's studies, an administrative position that would allow her to teach. This would be her first position that wasn't temporary and under someone else's direction. She wasn't sure she'd have too many more chances. She was old to be an assistant professor — one of the reasons she'd gone into administration in the first place. She thought she'd have a better chance there because she was older. In reality, however, she considered herself more a teacher than an administrator and this job combined both.

At first she'd been a little confused about how the system worked at this place. Even though it was tenure-track, she would be issued several short-term contracts and reviewed before she came up for tenure. She hoped that wouldn't be a problem; Lynn was sick of moving. They had moved so that Jessie could get her Ph.D., and now Lynn was following her around the country in her attempt to find a permanent university position.

She wanted to settle down. She didn't know how much longer they could afford to keep moving.

CHAPTER 2

Later that evening, Jessie and Lynn walked next door to the ancient, pieced-together faculty house, a house that had crude additions angling out in odd directions. Chris greeted them at the door. "Come in, come in. Here, let me introduce you. Carrie Small, history," she said, gesturing toward a woman thin to the point of anorexia who was sitting on the couch. "And her partner, Sandra. Jessie and Lynn." Chris smiled. "I believe you've met Denise Oberon and her partner Jennifer."

Jessie's started at the mention of Jennifer,

remembering Denise's denial during Jessie's interview visit.

A tall woman dressed in tan wool pants and a cream silk shirt came in from the kitchen. "This is my partner, Pam Effelton," Chris said. "Everyone else is in the kitchen. You'll notice that Joyce Barnette isn't here. We didn't invite her."

Those assembled in the living room gave each other knowing glances.

Some of the other factions became apparent that night. Jessie and Lynn ended up in the kitchen alone with Chris as they refilled their glasses.

Carrie said nervously, "I haven't been in the same room with Denise Oberon socially for a number of years."

"But aren't you in the same department? What happened?" Jessie asked.

Carrie took a sip of her wine. "Denise was wonderful to me when I first came to Burford. We were really good friends and spent a lot of time together. One day she decided that we were seeing too much of each other. Maybe Jennifer objected, I don't know, but after that she was distant. When review time came around for my contract, we had a horrible scene in her office. She was actually instructing me on how to teach her classes, and when I objected to her tone and started to leave, she ordered me to remain. I left anyway, and we've hardly spoken since."

When Jessie and Carrie returned to the living

room with their wine, Denise, who had left her dog at home, was petting Chris's little black mongrel. Pam's new dog, a Doberman pinscher puppy, lay on the floor next to the mongrel. Glancing around, Denise said, "Now you can see what it's like for lesbians at Burford. Pretty nice, hmm?"

"Why, Denise, you certainly didn't give that impression when you introduced me to Jennifer as your 'housemate.'" Jessie stopped, realizing that she'd embarrassed Denise.

Denise flushed, "Oh! I'm not always good with words. That's not what I meant to say."

Jessie saw Chris looking at her intently and the room became quiet.

Lynn broke the silence. "This cheesecake is very good. Who made it?"

"It's an old family recipe," Pam answered. "Would you like some more?" She rose, going to the table laden with desserts and beverages.

"Oh, no thanks. After all that rich food at the reception and now this . . ." Lynn shrugged.

"I heard you weren't feeling well this afternoon. Anything serious?" Jessie asked Pam.

"I get these migraines." Pam came over and sat down next to Chris on the couch. "Fortunately, I have some new medicine which seems to be working."

The dogs left the rocking chair where Denise was petting them and started to climb onto the couch. Chris and Pam moved over to make room.

"This is usually Susie's couch. She's so old that it's hard to deny her." Chris gestured toward the little black dog snuggling next to them. "Now that we have Betsy, we may have to rethink this. She'll

13

soon be too large," she said, pushing the puppy down and attempting to make her lie on the floor at their feet.

So, Jessie thought, here they were. She and Lynn were settled in a little faculty house at the bottom of the hill, next to the house of Chris Stendal and Pam Effelton. She wondered at the contradictions of the place — seeming open acceptance, a fractionized women's studies program and a nasty undertone of elitism, homophobia, sexism and even racism. Burford had a slick veneer all right; it prided itself on displaying a "liberal" front to the world. It celebrated its requirements for all students to take some sort of multicultural or women's studies class to graduate but required it's professors make those classes enjoyable, even amusing. Jessie couldn't believe she had been hired to present women's studies classes to such a hostile group. Her worst fear was that student ratings would be taken seriously when time for contract renewal rolled around.

Later that night, the siren positioned on a pole directly across from Jessie and Lynn's bedroom went off. Jessie jerked awake and Lynn reached over to calm her. "You're okay. It's just that goofy siren across the street. I can't believe in this day and age with beepers, they use this outdated system to call their emergency crews. I wonder what's going on."

The flashing lights shown into the bedroom as they went by, and Jessie got out of bed and peered out.

"They're going around the corner past Chris and

14

Pam's house. That's the street the stairs up the hill are on. Probably some drunken student had an accident."

"I wouldn't be surprised, since that's the drug of choice for these kids," Lynn replied. "Come back to bed."

Pulling the covers up, Jessie sighed. "Damn, I'll never get back to sleep now. My adrenalin is still rushing."

"Why don't you read for a while?" Lynn said as she turned on her side and her breathing seemed to indicate that she was already asleep.

CHAPTER 3

Sarah Brown, the part-time secretary Jessie and Chris shared, knocked on the open door of Jessie's office, and handed Jessie her mail. "Did you hear what happened last night?"

"You mean the sirens at two a.m.?" Jessie asked, glancing at the mail.

"Yes — " Sarah's voice wavered.

Concerned, Jessie looked up and waited.

"They found Joyce Barnette on the concrete stairs that run up the back of the hill. She fell, hit her head."

"Is she going to be all right?

"No, she's, she's . . . dead." Sarah blurted.

"Dead?" Jessie was aghast. After a shocked silence, she asked, "How do they think it happened? Do they think she slipped?" The steps were uneven, she knew. "I saw her heading up the hill after we left the reception, but I never dreamed . . ."

"They're saying it was no accident; they found a wire stretched across one of the steps." Sarah put her hands over her face and dropping her head, her gray pageboy falling over her hands.

Jessie waited for Sarah to compose herself, and then she said, "I know that Joyce was out of favor with the women's community, but who would hate her this much?"

Looking up, Sarah said, "All I know is there was a nasty battle last year. When the student came to Chris Stendal complaining about Joyce's behavior, they tried to fire Joyce. I always thought Chris went after Joyce a little too zealously, but murder?" Sarah's voice dropped. "I liked her. Before Chris came and all the uproar, she'd been very active in women's studies. This is awful," Sarah said, more to herself than Jessie as she turned and left the office, her yellow sweater disappearing around the door.

Jessie turned back to her desk full of paperwork, but she noticed a despondent-looking student in the hallway. She was tall and athletically built. She looked so miserable that the wall appeared to be holding her up. Jessie got up and poked her head out. "Are you looking for Chris Stendal? I don't think she's in yet. Is there something I can help you with? I'm the new Director of Women's Studies, Jessie Batelle."

The young woman looked up, pushing her short, shining blond hair out of her eyes. Jessie could see she'd been crying. She started crying again.

"Here, come into my office." Jessie grabbed a Kleenex from the box she kept for such emergencies. She handed it to the young woman. She took it and sank into one of Jessie's chairs, still sobbing. "Can you talk about it? Jessie asked.

"It's Joyce Barnette . . . I was the student who brought charges. You probably heard about it." She paused and looked at Jessie to see if she had to explain further. When Jessie nodded, she continued, "Joyce seemed so distant; I was afraid I was losing her. I needed to talk to someone and I'd seen Chris Stendal and Pam Effelton together and I knew Chris because she advises our feminist student group, so I came to Chris. Now that seems like a big mistake. Chris told me that Joyce had other women. I was so hurt and angry that it didn't take much to persuade me to file charges. I found out later that Chris wanted vengeance, but it was too late." Her voice trailed off again into sobs.

"And last night?" Jessie gently prodded.

"I was serving at the reception and I saw Joyce again. I saw Chris too. I wanted to tell Joyce how sorry I was. She said she'd be in her office after the reception. She always sets up her labs on Thursday evenings. But she wasn't there when I got off work. A note on the door said she'd had an emergency at home and now . . . You don't think they'll think I did it, do you?"

Before Jessie could answer, Chris walked by and the young woman jumped up and left. Jessie heard the door to Chris's office open and then close.

Through the wall, she could hear raised voices, but she couldn't make out the words. Jessie realized that she hadn't even learned the student's name.

She went back to her desk, turning to look out the window at the trees with their fall colors. She thought about Joyce's death. Not really sure why, she took out a notebook and began to make some notes. She didn't feel like doing much else anyway.

If the student's story was true, she and Lynn must have been two of the last people to see Joyce alive. Joyce had been running up the back steps about six. If she regularly set up her labs on Thursday nights as the student said, then anyone could have known she would be there. Obviously, it was planned. The wire must have been placed after Joyce went up the hill, Jessie thought, otherwise she would have tripped going up the hill when they were watching her. But she was taking two steps at a time. The note on the door seemed to suggest that someone called her and made sure she would hurry back down those steps. Could it have been the prankster group? What if someone just wanted to injure her and not kill her?

Remembering that Denise and Joyce had been involved and Chris's story from the other night, Jessie wondered if Denise could have failed to get her way and invented a new tactic. Was she that malignant? Wasn't this taking grudges too far? What about Chris and Pam? Jessie wrote down all the names she could come up with, thinking about motives and where they were at the time of death. But she realized she didn't know the time of death. Most of them were together at Chris's and Pam's party, unless Joyce died before or after the party. If it was before, it could have been any of the suspects. Any of them could have left the reception, set the wire, called Joyce and made sure she fell. Pam was the only one not at the reception, supposedly home ill. But the steps were very near her house.

Jessie put down her pen. The pranksters were an unknown quantity, but Jessie had heard that they usually were seen in masks and capes if they were pulling a prank. As far as she knew, no one had seen them.

CHAPTER 4

Later that day at home, Jessie found Lynn in the kitchen, chopping vegetables so intensely she hadn't heard her come in. Jessie said, "Hi, sweetie" and gave her a hug around her ample middle.

"Hmm, I missed you," she said.

"I don't know what I've gotten myself into. You know that siren last night? Joyce Barnette was murdered, coming down those back steps. Someone strung a wire across. She fell onto the rocks."

Lynn looked up from the cutting board. "What! Nice place we have here!" She put down the knife and turned to hug Jessie. Shorter than Jessie, she lay her head against Jessie's shoulder.

"You feel good. I've been wanting to be close to you all day," Jessie said, snuggling into her.

They stood there for a minute, then Lynn turned back to her vegetables. "What else have you heard about this?"

"Not much about the actual murder, but a lot about Joyce. She wasn't well liked by Chris who seems to have led a push to get Joyce fired for her involvement with a student. Chris doesn't make any secret of having been involved with Joyce and then dumped by her, though. Remember that scene at the reception last night? The woman Chris was talking to rather loudly was Joyce. Something was going on."

"Joyce was the one who almost knocked me down, going up the back steps to the campus?" Lynn asked thoughtfully.

"Right, and a few hours later she was dead," Jessie replied. "Apparently, Joyce had been involved with Denise too, so we have a nice incestuous lesbian mess. The student involved with all this happened into my office today. She was looking for Chris — blamed her for the death, I think. She felt she'd been tricked into filing charges by Chris. She said that she'd gone up to talk to Joyce at her office last evening, but that Joyce had been called away. She never saw her."

"I don't like the looks of this. I suppose you were hired to calm this situation down. Bring in an outsider. Well, not much hope of that now. It's gone too far. Not that you could have done anything about it, all these factions." Lynn shook her head.

"No," Jessie said. "I'm beginning to get

frightened. There are so many divisions. It's hard to figure out who to trust. I'm the untenured one, and all their opinions count. Who knows what I'm really supposed to be doing —"

Lynn cut in. "It's not much in comparison to murder, but I had a bad day too. I was working on the bookshelves out in the side yard and some guy from this quaint neighborhood walked right up to me and said, 'Hey, what are you doing? Sawing? I didn't know women could do that.' At first I thought he was kidding, but he wasn't."

Jessie munched a carrot from the pile of vegetables. "How old was this guy?"

"Oh, in his thirties, I guess. A little younger than us."

"What did you say to him?"

"I told him thank you very much, women did such things all the time. He left, but I was so angry I felt like braining him with my hammer. Good thing he didn't stick around," Lynn said vehemently. "I hate living in this neighborhood. People watch everything you do, and they feel they have the right to comment. What bullshit!"

Jessie laughed. "Ah, now I see why the vigorous chopping — you were imagining it was this guy, and maybe some of the nosy neighbors, hmm? Our work on the lawn and putting in some plants certainly has gotten noticed. I suppose the townspeople don't really like having these faculty rental houses here. Faculty come and go pretty quickly — maybe even quicker than we imagined if today is any example — and probably don't spend a lot of time keeping up the property. This one must have looked pretty bad before they re-sided it."

Jessie grimaced with pain at the kitten attempting to climb her pantleg. "Who's this? Where did she — is it a she? — come from?"

"Oh, I forgot to tell you. Seems the neighbor across the street takes in strays. She has about all the animals she can handle right now so she asked if we'd take it. She said we looked like we were good to our animals. I felt sorry for the little tyke. She said its littermate was killed climbing into a truck engine for warmth. I said we'd try it," she said apologetically. "and yes, it's a female."

Jessie picked up the gray tiger-striped kitten. "Well, hello." She looked at Lynn and said, "How have the big cats been with her? They were pretty upset last time we brought home a kitten."

"They've been okay," Lynn said. "I think they're still disoriented from moving and haven't properly established their territory."

"It's strange living in a house that's had a succession of faculty. Did you know the last woman was only in here a year? Chris told me she hated Burford. Went to Yale from here. I guess the old guys in her department made life miserable for her. I hear they have several departments in which women have a really rough time. She was lucky to get out of here on her own terms, though, given the academic market," Jessie mused. The kitten batted at her swinging earrings. "I wonder what part Chris plays in the problems women have on campus? She seems to be a favorite of the president, and from what I've seen she does a good job with the center. One thing bothers me, though. I thought we were supposed to work together on the programming. Remember that letter I got requesting suggestions? Now Chris says it's all done and none of my ideas are in the schedule. The way the program is set up she's supposed to be my closest ally. Actually, I bet the only reason she doesn't have my position is that she hasn't finished her Ph.D."

"There's something not quite right about her. I don't think you should trust her. You *are* too trusting, part of your military brat openness," Lynn said. She dropped her diced vegetables into the frying pan.

"Stir fry for dinner? Smells good. How did the job search go?" Jessie said sniffing appreciatively.

"Well, there's a legal advocacy position in a battered women's shelter about thirty miles from here. I start in a couple of weeks," Lynn said, stirring the vegetables. "The pay is about ten grand less than I made before, though."

"Congratulations! So we should be celebrating. Too bad about the pay, but it's not like I got a big raise to come here," Jessie said. "I guess it can't be helped in such a rural area. Once again, you come up with a job almost effortlessly while I send out hundreds of applications."

"Oh well, there are battered women everywhere."

"And not too many advocates who have the skills you do. The academic market is really tight." All those years to get a Ph.D. and so few jobs, she thought. So much for the market opening up in the '90s. With the budget cuts, a lot of universities weren't even replacing retirements. She was lucky to have this position, given her age and all those temporary jobs. This was the first one which might be permanent.

Lynn frowned. "I just don't know how long I can

stand living in this village with everyone poking their noses into our business. If we're going to stay here, we're going to have to find somewhere else to live."

"I know — as soon as we recover financially from the move. But I don't feel like I'll have too many more chances — gray-haired assistant professors aren't exactly popular," Jessie said, sighing.

"You aren't gray. I look years older than you do, even though I'm not," Lynn said, touching her gray curls. "But I know what you mean. It would be nice to settle down," she added reassuringly.

"I hope we won't be sorry we came here. I'm beginning to wish I hadn't taken this job so quickly. I should've kept interviewing. I realize now that I know nothing about private university culture," Jessie said, trying to rescue her earring from the kitten. She glanced at the clock on the tiny kitchen's wall. "Oh! I have to hurry. Will dinner be ready soon? I've been wanting to meet some of the students who are interested in women's issues. Chris advises the group, and they're meeting not far from here, just up at the top of the hill behind us, actually. Chris didn't seem too eager to have me, so I hope I'm not treading on her territory. I told her I'd meet her up there."

As she put the lid on the steaming vegetables, Lynn said, "Dinner will be ready in about ten minutes. Why don't you grab those plates? What time is the meeting?"

Jessie put the kitten down, restored her earring and took plates out of the cupboard. She took them a few steps into the small dining area. "It's at seven. Chris says that not many come regularly, so she doesn't know whether they'll be more than a few.

Oh! She showed me a really ugly flyer that the prankster group put out in honor of Gay and Lesbian Awareness Week. I had the honor of being one of the features — Joyce and I were supposed to be 'teaching' lesbian sex classes with demonstrations, yet! They also featured the Dean of Students whom they apparently don't like. Chris said that the President and her family were featured in one right after she arrived. You don't suppose they had anything to do with Joyce's death, do you? Want to see it?"

Lynn nodded. Jessie went to her briefcase and removed the black and white, letter-sized flyer. Lynn frowned as she strained to read the badly printed sheet. "This is really ugly! Since this isn't the first one, what has the administration tried to do about it? This might qualify for prosecution under a hate crimes law."

Well, there are First Amendment issues, but so far, I guess they haven't been able to catch anyone. One of my students had a message on her answering machine from a printer that the flyers were ready , but her roommates erased it as a wrong number without getting the name. After the flyer came out, the student put it together and mentioned it during a class discussion. If they had the name of the printer, they could have found out who placed the order." Jessie sat down at the table. "What was amazing to me, though, was how scared this student was. When pressed, she insisted that she really didn't know anything and that she didn't want word to get out that she had said anything. According to her, these guys, who are supposed to come from the social elite of Burford, could make her a social outcast while she's here at Burford. There must be some way of getting the women to link up and take back some of their power on this campus."

Jessie reached over and lifted the calico cat down to the floor. The cat immediately sat and begin bathing herself casually.

Lynn shook her head. "From what you tell me, the women here never had much power. They can't live in their sorority houses, and they care too darn much about pleasing the men on this campus. I thought that attitude was outdated, but this little college seems to be a bastion of male privilege. Women's Studies is certainly needed here, but it looks like you won't be serving the women. Your task seems to be to educate the men."

"A real irony," Jessie said. "And I wanted so much to teach women about their own heritage and give them a safe space to explore — try to do that in the presence of twenty sullen fraternity boys taking the class as a requirement."

"And how frightening for the women if you teach them to question their position! Since the male attitude reigns, I think you'll just be a token here. You can't last very long — the men won't like your message and they'll chalk up their discomfiture to 'bad teaching,' the standard dismissal of a 'teaching' college when a faculty member doesn't toe the line. Mustn't upset these little rich kids. After all, they pay the bills." Lynn went into the kitchen and started dishing up the food, slamming a cupboard door out of her way.

Jessie followed her. "Don't you think the women will protect me? You don't think they understand?"

The gray velour cat jumped to the counter and

headed toward the food. Lynn grabbed the water squirter and aimed. The cat flinched and leaped down.

"From what I know about Carrie and Denise and the silence at the party when I criticized Denise — well, maybe I shouldn't think they *will* back me," Jessie said. "The problem is that most of the women are also untenured and see themselves as pretty powerless. I think they expect me, an untenured director, to be powerful for them. The only way I think it'll work is if we act in coalition."

Lynn put up her hand. "Stop. Remind me who Denise is. I've only seen her once, you know, if at all."

"Oh, sorry. Denise was the chair of the search committee, a full professor and apparently doesn't like her authority challenged. Remember at the party, she talked about what a wonderful place Burford is for lesbian faculty? She has light brown wavy hair, post earrings, preppy? Carrie's in Denise's department. Thin, nervous. We met her at the party. She's real California, matching pants and top with applique on them. She was the one really upset with being in the same room as Denise," Jessie said, seeing a gleam of recognition come into Lynn's green eyes.

"Speaking of authority," Jessie said, "I met Georgia Swain today. She has the office just down the hall from me. She's one of the few women full professors besides Denise. She wants to meet me on the bike trail sometime later next week to fill me in on her version of the lesbian community. She says she rides the bike trail regularly to keep her girlish figure. She was a really good friend of Joyce's and thinks she might have some clues to the murder.

She's just come back from two years of leave." Jessie reached down and petted the gray cat who was sitting staring at the counter. "It turns out that Georgia is really a baby dyke." Fell in love during her leave with a woman dean elsewhere and now is discovering herself as lesbian. She's enthusiastic and the administration is trotting her out as their pet lesbian to show that they aren't biased. Butter wouldn't melt in her mouth most of the time. She's got a case of 'I've never been discriminated against at Burford so it must be all right.' "

Lynn delivered the food to the table and sat down. "Was that the woman dressed *Vogue*-dyke style at the reception — tailored pants and vest?"

Sitting down across from her, Jessie said, "That's the one. She also mentioned to me that Joyce used to be really active in women's studies. What she thinks was a silly feud between Chris and Joyce occurred while she was gone. Georgia's pretty astonished at all this. She wants to get to the bottom of what happened. She doesn't seem to have any love lost over Chris, though, and Chris would have been hired during Georgia's absence. I wonder if she thinks Chris had something to do with Joyce's death. I guess Georgia was never active in women's studies. She left that up to everybody else, so all this is new to her.

She wasn't at the party. I wonder if that means Chris considers her an enemy or she just had another engagement."

Jessie broke off as the gray cat made another try — this time for the food on the table. "Darn, where are your manners! You've certainly forgotten them since the move. A fine example you are for the new kitten!" Jessie went to the kitchen for the squirter.

Lynn put down her fork and put her hand out to guard Jessie's food. "From your description of her, she certainly seems to fit right into the faculty here — right into the faculty sorority system, that is, a real Southern lady."

"She seems to mean well," Jessie said as she sat down with the squirter. Just the appearance of the squirter made the cat jump down and head for cover.

Jessie grabbed a last bite, put down her fork and pushed her chair out. "Look at the time. I've got to hurry."

"Isn't the place you're going just above where Joyce was killed?" Lynn asked.

"Yes, I guess it is. I haven't been there yet."

"Well, be careful. Take the car. I love you," Lynn said as Jessie went for her coat.

CHAPTER 5

It was already dark when Jessie parked her car on the shoulder of the road circling the campus near what she guessed to be the community center for student housing. She walked over to the top of the stairs descending the hill and looked down. The area was cordoned off by yellow police tape, a reminder of last night's events. The steps were only wide enough for a single pedestrian and the only way up or down on this side of the campus. By car one would have to go all the way around. The steps were lit fairly well, but Jessie could see how a wire would have been invisible. She could see a dark streak on the big boulder about a quarter of the way down where Joyce must have landed. She shuddered and turned away toward the community center.

Inside the dimly lit room was a kind of snack bar. A couple of male students sat at a corner booth. Jessie ordered a soft drink from the student behind the counter and sat down at a table to wait. After what seemed like an eternity, a couple of young women came in.

"Are you here for the women's meeting?" Jessie asked.

They both had long, blond, straight hair and were carefully made up to look as if they weren't wearing makeup. The one with the longest hair said yes and Jessie introduced herself. After they had ordered, she asked them what projects they had been working on.

"We're planning a women's week in the spring and next month, a reproductive rights speakout on the quad at lunch. We'll be sending around a notice soon to invite the campus to come and speak out," one of them replied.

Just then Chris came in with her olive raincoat and her trademark purple book bag. Pam trailed in after her. Jessie had been told that Pam was still in graduate school and was known for her athletic ability. Nearly six feet tall, she had played basketball and had been good enough to get a scholarship at the state university. Now that she had graduated, she spent her days playing golf when she wasn't at the university. She had won quite a name for herself in the local women's circuit. Jessie had seen her jogging around town and on the bike path which stretched from town to town along the abandoned railroad tracks.

Unlike Chris, who still retained a casual graduate-school style of sweatshirts and jeans, Pam wore tailored blazers and wool pants. She looked as if she belonged at Burford, given her expensive, tasteful clothes. Jessie wondered how Pam felt about Joyce's death since Chris and Joyce had been involved at one point. What did the conversation between Chris and Joyce at the reception mean? "I told you. Stay away from her! I won't have this start again," Chris had said. Had Joyce been threatening Chris and Pam's relationship in some way? Or had Chris seen Joyce talking to the student who brought the sexual harassment charges and was trying once again to intervene? Of course, Jessie couldn't ask.

Chris and Pam came over and Chris said, "I'm sorry I'm late. The whole day has been full of dealing with Joyce's death."

"Were lots of students upset?" Jessie asked.

One of the blond students replied, "Oh yes, that's why this meeting is so small. Lots of us have had Dr. Barnette for class. It doesn't seem possible that she's dead."

"You won't catch me near those steps," the other chimed in. "I used to use them to get down to the pizza parlor on that side — no more."

Chris pulled out a chair and said, "And our house is on that side — Jessie's, too.

The students got up and went off to get refills of their drinks and Jessie asked, "Did you hear anything before the siren went off last night?"

"No, we'd just gotten to bed and fallen asleep after cleaning up after the party. We were pretty tired," Chris replied.

"They think Joyce was killed early — between six-thirty and seven — so we wouldn't have heard anything," Pam said. "Chris was on her way home from the reception, and I was running errands getting ready for the party."

"You know, Lynn and I were probably the last people to see her. She ran up the back steps right in front of us about six. But it's pretty dark on that side of the hill in the trees — the lights weren't on by then — so we didn't see anything unusual. Of course, we haven't been here long enough to know what might be unusual."

Pam shifted her long legs and said, "I'm sure the police will be interested to know that you were one of the last to see her."

"Oh, by the way, thanks for the party. It was nice to meet everyone," Jessie said.

Chris said, "I was glad to see you stand up to Denise Oberon last night. I told myself, well, good, Jessie isn't afraid of her. She *is* one of the few women full professors on campus."

"I gather from Carrie that I have something to be afraid of," Jessie said, taking a sip of her coffee.

"Yes, Carrie's had a bad time," Chris said.

"What will that mean when tenure time comes around? Will Denise oppose her tenure?" Jessie asked.

"Well, Carrie passed her last review. She's on leave now, bringing her publishing up to snuff. She should be okay."

That personality and perception might play a

bigger part in tenure than anything else was a rather ominous idea, but Jessie didn't pursue it any further, just noted it for the future.

"You know, Chris didn't even get to meet you before you were hired. Can you imagine two positions that are supposed to work together so closely and not letting her have a say in your hiring?" Pam said with surprising vehemence. "We thought we'd like to get to know you better by having a party," she added.

Just then the students came back and the conversation shifted to the business of the day.

When Jessie came out of the building, a fog had risen and the place looked even eerier. She pulled her gray raincoat in closer. As she approached her car, she saw that there was something on the windshield. She lifted the wiper and picked up what appeared to be a flyer. She unlocked her car and leaned in to look at the soggy flyer by the dome light. It was a copy of the same ugly flyer which she had shown Lynn earlier, only this time her name was circled in red marker. "You're next! Leave now!" was scrawled in big red letters. Joyce Barnette's name was crossed out with a skull over her name.

Jessie dropped the flyer into the car as if she'd been scalded. She hastily looked around, slammed and locked her doors. She thought she heard laughter coming from around the building. She was shaking as she started her car. She wanted to get out of there as fast as possible. If this was a joke of the prankster group, it wasn't funny. It had gone way too far.

On the way down the hill, the headlights revealed

only dark forms shrouded in thick fog. Jessie had trouble staying on the road. She turned a corner too sharply and ran over the curb. She tried to calm herself. She told herself it was only a little farther. She anguished over what to do.

Part of the legacy of being a military brat was that she hated to make a scene. For instance, she put off going to the doctor as long as possible until she was sure she was really sick because she didn't want to be embarrassed if it turned out to be nothing. She probably wasn't in any immediate danger, she thought. If it were the murderer, why give her warning? Whoever it was probably just wanted to scare her. She'd see what Lynn thought, she decided as she pulled up in front of the house and saw the welcoming porch light.

Lynn had gone to a movie and wasn't home yet, and as Jessie got ready for bed, she kept hearing a meow. She couldn't figure out where it was coming from. Could one of the cats have gotten into her dresser? It sounded like the kitten. She pulled open her drawers one by one, but nothing. She opened the closet and peered in — no kitten.

"Here, kitty, kitty," she called.

A plaintive meow was all she got. She heard Lynn come home and slam the door.

"Lynn, would you come up here?" she said, exasperated.

Jessie went to the window and peered out onto the porch roof. Had the kitten gotten out and onto the roof? The meows seemed to follow her around the room. She tried the closet again and the meows followed her into it.

Lynn came into the room. "What's the matter?"

"Listen," Jessie said. "I can't figure out where that meowing is coming from. I've looked in my drawers, the closet and even out the windows on the porch roof. Where do you think it's coming from?"

Lynn called, "Kitty, kitty," and listened for a moment. "It seems to be coming from under the windows. Try walking back toward the closet and call her again."

Jessie walked back over to the closet, opened the door and called again. The meow came from under her feet.

"She's under the floorboards," Lynn said.

"Under the floorboards? How on earth?" Jessie was baffled.

"Let's see if one of the boards is loose," Lynn said. She went into the closet and began pulling at the boards. "I'll have to get a crowbar. Just keep her here by calling every once in a while. At least we know the wiring is in pretty good shape. She's not electrocuted. She must have gone in that space between the wall and the furnace duct when I had the storage room open earlier," she said, shaking her head at the folly of kittens.

"Can't we just call her back to the duct and let her crawl out instead of pulling up the floorboards?" Jessie asked.

"We don't know if she'd be able to get back there. No use risking her hitting a bad wire," Lynn offered. "Taking up a board or two in the closet won't show much.

While Lynn was gone to look for the crowbar, Jessie sat on the floor by the open closet door, crooning to the kitten who answered with sad little meows.

When Lynn came back with the crowbar, a flashlight and some kitty treats, she pried up a couple of boards. "Okay, you grab her while I try to coax her over with these treats."

The kitten stuck her head out and Jessie swooped her up. "My, look at you. You're filthy!" The kitten's white stripes had turned gray, muting the tiger effect and making her look as if she was a solid, dark gray.

Lynn took the kitten and said, "Bath for you. Your reward for being a curious cat!"

A few minutes later she brought in the indignant kitten wrapped in a towel and put her on the bed. Jessie sighed, "She's the worst ever for getting into trouble. What are we going to do with her?"

Lynn glanced up at her. "You seem upset. Is it the kitten?"

Jessie shook her head. "No, I found a threatening flyer on my windshield this evening. It's still in the car. I didn't even want to touch it."

"Threatening?"

"Yes, it was one of those flyers I showed you earlier, but my name had a 'You're next! Leave now!' written by it, and the line through Joyce's name had a skull next to it."

"Given that Joyce has just been murdered, I think we should call the police," Lynn said.

"Maybe I should turn it over to security first — give the college a chance to handle it. It *is* a flyer from the prankster group. Maybe this will convince the president to do something about them," Jessie said.

"Yeah, right. I bet they just bury it — bad publicity," Lynn said with a cynical sneer.

CHAPTER 6

When she got to the office the next morning, Jessie talked to Sarah about the flyer, and Sarah called security. About a half-hour later, a small, uniformed man appeared in her doorway.

"I'm Bob Martin, security. Your secretary called about a problem?" he said, walking briskly into the room with an air of self-importance.

"Yes, I found this on my windshield last night," Jessie said, getting up from her desk and handing him the flyer.

Bob glanced at it with its big red message. Jessie

saw him look up at her, seeming a little startled by her height. He took a big breath of air and sort of puffed himself up to appear taller. "Where was your car at the time?"

"Parked on the road near the residence hall community center where I was attending a meeting," Jessie said.

"And what time did you find the flyer?"

"It must have been about eight-thirty," Jessie said, noticing that the man was having difficulty maintaining his attempt at appearing taller and had to let out his breath.

"Did you see anyone suspicious?" he asked with sort of a squeak as the air rushed out.

"No, the place was deserted except for the few of us coming out of the meeting." Jessie smiled, unable to suppress her amusement at him.

"Do you have any idea who would have put this on your car?" he said, his face turning red from embarrassment at his squeak.

"No, no one I can think of."

Bob recovered his composure and said, "You haven't had any disagreements with any students, then — poor test grades or content of your classes?"

Jessie thought for a minute, then answered, "If anyone was this unhappy, they haven't told me about it."

"Well, I'll look into this and pass the information on to the officers investigating Dr. Barnette's death in case there is any connection. It might be more of the pranksters' mischief. President Whiffle is having fits about the bad publicity. You might want to be discreet about who you tell about this so as not to upset the community any further," he commented.

She started to say something about his taking the flyer, but the little man had turned abruptly and left. Today in the sunlight the flyer didn't seem as threatening as it had last night. She remembered Lynn's notion that if she waited to report it through Burford, they'd try to keep the lid on it so as not to upset the rich little students and their parents who pay the bills. Jessie hadn't believed it, but here it was.

Just then, Chris popped into her office. "Sarah told me you'd been threatened," she said with excitement. "Can I see it?"

"Bob Martin took it," Jessie answered. "It was the same ugly flyer that came out last week, only this time my name was circled in red and a big 'You're next' was scrawled on it. Do you think it's serious? Bob seemed to think that it just might be the prankster group again."

"It's hard to say. They *are* fearless. Rumor is that the leaders are mostly sons of powerful alumni. So far no one knows who they are for sure, but membership is supposed to be like a legacy. They used to do annoying pranks, like putting a donkey in the library, but for the past couple of years, they've really targeted groups and individuals who threaten to change their fraternity world. Feminists are a favorite target. Last year they broke into the desk in the Women's Center where our stationery is kept and sent out a terrible memo on our letterhead." Chris played with the pink triangle magnet on Jessie's file cabinet.

"You didn't see anyone suspicious when you and Pam came out of the meeting last night, did you?" Jessie asked.

"No, no one seemed to be around. From my house, I usually walk and use the stairs, but Pam and I drove. The stairs were blocked off anyway." Chris let the magnet go with a snap.

"Do people know you regularly use those stairs? Could that wire have been put there for someone else? Who else uses the stairs?" In military-brat style, questions rushed out of her.

"Well, yes, it's common knowledge I use the stairs in good weather. They *are* right behind my house. Only a few faculty live on this side of the hill close enough to use the stairs — Joyce, of course, me, you, Denise. Everyone else lives too far to use them regularly." Chris checked her watch. "Well, I've got a meeting to go to. Talk to you later." With that she disappeared as quickly as she had come.

That afternoon Jessie saw Georgia Swain briefly in the hall. She looked particularly spiffy in a yellow-flowered man's tie, vest and long skirt. She was using her little pink triangle pin as a tie tack. Since she had come back, she had taken it upon herself to be open in all her classes. Wearing the pink triangle had been one way of doing that. They were handed out every year during Gay and Lesbian Awareness Week to anyone who would take one. As a result most students knew what they meant.

"Oh, I'm glad I ran into you," Georgia said. "Can you meet me at the bike trail on the bridge where it goes across the creek at four on Monday? I've uncovered some things that you might want to know, but I don't have time now. Someone might be listening," she whispered mysteriously.

Jessie thought she'd wait to tell Georgia about the flyer then.

That weekend Jessie and Lynn went to a party at Lucy Taft's house. Jessie had to call Lucy and ask how to get to her house since there seemed to be no map of the village. Lucy had a large sprawling house on a cul de sac. When Jessie and Lynn arrived the guests were already spilling out onto the front porch. Lucy's department was a large one and when Jessie was directed to choose to affiliate with a department besides women's studies, she had chosen Lucy's.

Looking a bit harried, Lucy greeted them at the door. "Come in, come in. Main dishes go on the table. Desserts in the kitchen."

Jessie took their store-bought pie to the kitchen, grumbling to herself about potlucks. Was she supposed to have time and inclination to cook? She eyed the display of dishes cooked up by the assembled women and felt as if she couldn't compete. Was she supposed to ask Lynn to play the role of wife and contribute? She noticed the other store-bought dish was being set on the table by an unmarried male faculty member.

She and Lynn got some wine and tried to mingle. They were talking to Ralph, a balding professor who was carrying on about how homogenous a group the Burford faculty were. Before she thought, Jessie asked, "How do you think Joyce fit into that? Did she fit in here?"

Lynn gave her a sharp look. Ralph sort of stuttered. Just then Lucy called from the dining room that people should come and get their food.

They took their food out on to the porch where Georgia sat. Jessie made the introductions as they settled themselves on the porch railing.

"I really miss Joyce." Georgia sighed. "Even though she was from a different department, we always invited her. She always said we had the best potlucks. You're still meeting me on Monday, aren't you, Jessie?"

Jessie nodded, and Lucy came out with her plate to join them.

"I've been meaning to tell you, Jessie, that you need to teach our freshman introductory course sometime. I was reminded by some of our department that we decided a long time ago if anyone affiliated with us, they would have to teach the freshman introductory course, not just their specialties."

"But my assignment is really women's studies," Jessie said, surprised. "And I have to teach the introductory women's studies course every semester. Teaching another introductory course will cut down on any upper division women's studies courses I could offer. I thought the hiring committee wanted the women's studies curriculum beefed up."

"It's not my idea," she said. "Talk to Ralph. He's the one who brought it up. I'm just the messenger."

The conversation continued, but Jessie didn't hear much. She was thinking about this turn of events. One of the pluses of this position was that she was to teach entirely women's studies courses. How could they change this on her now? She knew that Lucy was a new department chair, and she had heard that it was because no one else wanted to do it. Lucy wasn't considered to be the best choice. Was she afraid to support Jessie against the men in the department? Did they still hold the power?

CHAPTER 7

On Monday, Jessie rode her bike the few blocks from her house through the small Victorian village to the bike trail. She entered the trail off the main road and steered behind the feed store to where the asphalt path became more isolated. The sounds of traffic became muffled and birds could be heard calling in the quiet. The smell of wet leaves and damp earth was strong. The trail had been built alongside the old railroad tracks. Trees sheltered the path. On one side, green lawns butted the trees, changing into fields with an occasional cow as Jessie rode along, the breeze stirring her hair. On the other side were woods and a creek which the trail would eventually cross over.

Several women students jogged by in the opposite direction, heading back to Burford. It was strange, but she never saw male students jogging on the path. They seemed to favor the athletic facilities at Burford.

As Jessie rounded a curve, she saw Pam ride by, going back toward town. She seemed a little startled to see Jessie as she sped by on her expensive-looking bike. Oddly, she had a golf club with her. Jessie waved and continued on. The day was sunny and pleasant, the temperature in the 60s. The bright, falling leaves made the path a little slippery where they had piled up in yesterday's rain. As Jessie neared the place where the bike path crossed over the creek, both sides of the trail became more wooded and isolated. She felt happy to be out of her office enjoying the fall, especially after the events of the past week. Thankfully, the trail was flat. She had a ten-speed bike with wide tires, but she hadn't gotten used to shifting the gears. She usually left the bike in one gear if she could.

By the time she neared the place she was to meet Georgia, her butt was falling asleep. This was a not-too-unpleasant sensation when she stopped and rested for a minute, watching the creek swollen from yesterday's rain. She remembered the women's studies director from her last position telling her gleefully about how her husband had taken a long bike ride. His genitals had fallen asleep. He had had a lot of trouble restoring his circulation. Jessie smiled to herself.

She'd lost track of time, and when she looked at her watch, it was after four. Georgia was nowhere to be seen on the trail ahead or behind. In fact, there was no one around. The path curved around a bend before the bridge where they were to meet, so Jessie decided to go on. Georgia might be waiting just out of sight.

As she approached the bridge, she noticed a break in the piling leaves which went off the path and down the embankment as if something had scraped or been dragged through. She got off her bike and looked down. Near the creek was a bike and its rider. She couldn't see any movement.

"Georgia!" she yelled, dropping her bike and scrambling down the embankment, sliding and falling on the slippery leaves. She lost her balance and plummeted into a rock outcropping. Pain shot through her knee as she grabbed at the bushy undergrowth to stop herself from going head first down the rest of the way. She felt her way gingerly the rest of the way, grabbing stocky twigs to keep her balance. Her knee was throbbing.

Georgia lay tangled with her bike — one arm twisted in a manner that made Jessie wince. Jessie leaned close to see if there were any signs of life, touching Georgia softly at first and then more firmly while calling her name. She didn't stir. She didn't seem to be breathing. Jessie yanked Georgia's head back and began mouth-to-mouth. Silently counting she inhaled, blew into Georgia's lungs, looked away and exhaled. After five minutes, Jessie knew her efforts were useless.

Shaken, Jessie looked around at the suddenly ominous trees which seemed to leer over her and heard the sounds of the creek rushing by a few yards away. She yelled for help and her words echoed back at her mockingly. She realized if this hadn't been an accident, she had probably already destroyed any clues as she had tumbled down the embankment. It wasn't going to be that easy to get out, either. Before coming down she hadn't paid much attention to how steep it really was.

As she looked back at Georgia's lifeless body, she noticed that Georgia's sweater was ripped up by the neck where she usually wore her little pink triangle. The triangle was gone. She looked closer. Georgia's neck was muddy under the rip. She thought it must have come off early in the fall or before the fall. She pulled herself together to go for help. The bank was so steep and slick with mud she had to pull herself up by grabbing small trees and brush. Twice she lost her footing and slipped down, catching herself on a clump of brush. Once she had slid into the track made by Georgia's bike and had plummeted down the hillside almost landing on top of the body. When she finally got to the top, she was covered with mud. She had to get on her bike and ride the half mile or so to where the trail came out. She knew there were a few stores across the road where she could go. Trying to control her shaking and ignore the pain in her knee, she pedaled weakly toward the road.

CHAPTER 8

Jessie called the police from a convenience store once she had gotten to the road. Since she couldn't stand on her leg with her bad knee by the time the patrol car arrived, the cops didn't make her walk back to where Georgia lay at the bottom of the bank. Muddy and upset, Jessie waited for them in the squad car in the bike trail parking lot. Finally, the officer made his way back to the car. Jessie heard him call for a team to bring out the body. Then he turned to Jessie, "I'll run you home, ma'am. She's dead, all right. I'll take your statement when we get to your house. You live on College Avenue?"

Jessie nodded and sank back into her seat, closing her eyes. She felt numb except for the throbbing pain in her knee. When they pulled up in front of her house, Jessie could see that it was late enough that Lynn was already home. She came out and helped Jessie up the steep front stairs with the officer following.

"What happened?" she asked, the concern sounding in her voice.

"I went to meet Georgia and found her and her bicycle at the bottom of the bank near the bridge on the bike trail," Jessie explained.

"Is she okay?"

"She's dead." Jessie responded in a flat voice, stepping into the small living room where Lynn helped her to the couch.

"You look as if you should be going to the hospital, ma'am." The officer took out a small notepad.

"I'll take her," Lynn said.

"If I could get your statement now, I'll be on my way. You say you found Ms. Swain about four-thirty? How do you know that was the time?"

"I was supposed to meet her at that spot at about four. I remember looking at my watch because she was late and I didn't see her anywhere."

"What happened after you looked at your watch?"

"I went to the bridge and noticed a disturbance in the leaves on the path. I saw Georgia and her bike at the bottom of the embankment. I called to her and went down the bank to see if she was all right since she didn't answer. She was dead," she said quietly. "I tried mouth-to-mouth."

"Did you see anyone else or anything else you should tell me about?"

"No, there was no one around. Georgia's body was all twisted . . ." she said and began to cry.

Jessie had trouble sleeping that night, and in the morning she was so shaken up that she cancelled her classes and stayed home. Her knee had swelled to huge proportions until she could not put weight on her left leg, and Lynn didn't have to work very hard to convince her to let her take her to the emergency room. There was an ambulance blocking the emergency room door, and they had to park some distance away. Jessie leaned on Lynn's sturdy frame and hopped across the parking lot.

She was sorry she'd come. If she'd been able to walk, she would have gotten up and left. The emergency area was full of burn victims, small children and mothers crying. She could hear a man cursing in a slurred voice in the curtained-off cubicle next to her. The nurse told her that he was drunk and had jumped off the roof of a two-story building. When the alcohol wore off he would be saying worse things.

Jessie felt faint.

Lynn looked at her and said, "Breathe."

Finally, after x-rays, they gave her a foam-covered brace with Velcro straps and crutches and told her not to put weight on her left leg. She wasn't very good at going up and down the stairs on crutches. At the risk of her job, Lynn had stayed home with her the first few days. Jessie tried to work on the revisions to her book manuscript, but under the circumstances, she found it difficult to concentrate on *The Promise of Women's Communities in Academe.* She spent most of her time propped up in bed watching daytime television with the cats.

Gremlin, the gray cat, always climbed under the heavy comforter and lay next to her legs while the calico and the kitten vied for her lap. The loser would lay next to her legs on the outside until Jessie felt as if there were sandbags weighing her down and she would shoo the cats away. When she had to go downstairs, she would slide down on her butt, using her crutches again at the foot of the stairs. Fortunately, there was a bathroom both up and down.

The weather was nasty most of the time. She had no incentive to try to go outside. She thought it was odd that no one but her secretary called or came by during the week and a half she was home, but mostly she was so upset and depressed that she didn't care. Joyce's death had been a murder, but Georgia's was ruled an accident. Jessie couldn't believe it, though, and she spent part of her time adding to her notes. She tried to figure out who would have known Georgia was going to meet her that day on the bike trail. She remembered that Georgia had mentioned it at least twice to her — once in front of Chris's office and again at the party. Jessie herself had told Lynn, but she hadn't stated the time, so if Lynn had said anything to anyone, they wouldn't have known the time. Of course, Georgia could have told someone else.

Toward the end of the first week, home from work, Lynn came into the bedroom where Jessie lay hemmed in by the cats. Oprah was on.

"Would you believe this?" Jessie said. "Oprah's thin again. I've been watching this all week and I just noticed."

Lynn shook her head. "That must mean you're feeling better. You've been in a fog most of the time. I've been really worried about you. I've got chicken for supper. Are you hungry?"

"I guess so. Do you want me to get up?"

"No, stay where you are. I've got plans for you after dinner." Lynn smiled.

"Plans?" Jessie smiled back at her. She shooed the cats, then said, "What am I going to do about Lucy's threat to have me teach the department's introductory course if I want their support? I was going to ask Georgia about it, but she was dead before I had a chance to talk to her. She was the only faculty member in the department with any power besides the old boys whose idea this seems to be."

"I don't know. What about calling the Women's Studies Committee together and getting their advice? Why are you affiliated with Lucy's department anyway?" Lynn responded.

"I was told that the place was so small that I should be connected with some department besides the women's studies program, but that gives me an idea. Rather than give in to this blackmail, maybe I should unaffiliate. It really seems like a way of controlling me and the Women's Studies Program. It frosts me that Lucy is part of the Women's Studies

Committee and she gave in to the old boys in her department. It's not right!"

"Ah, you are feeling better. I hear that military sense of injustice in your voice," Lynn said with a smile.

Lynn went back downstairs to fix dinner. It occurred to Jessie that she must look pretty terrible. She pushed the cats off the bed yet again and used her crutches to get herself into the bathroom to wash up and brush her hair, surprised to find that she was interested in Lynn's "plan." By the time Lynn came up with a tray for her, she had washed, combed her hair, put on a clean nightshirt and deodorant.

"Well, you are looking better." Lynn set down the tray on her lap.

While Jessie ate, Lynn teased her by nibbling on her neck and lightly touching her exposed skin.

"Stop! You're giving me goosebumps!" Jessie protested.

"Good, it's about time I got some response from you." Lynn took the tray and put it on the corner of the dresser. She chased the cats out and closed the door. "No chicken bones for cats," she told them. She took off her clothes and came over to Jessie, pulling off her nightshirt and gently easing her down on the bed so as not to hurt her knee. She lay next to Jessie, stroking and kissing her nipples, then biting at them until they tingled. She reached down and continued stroking until Jessie had forgotten her knee and was writhing in pleasure. Finally, Jessie arched her back, her breath coming in gasps. She pulled Lynn down to her and the stroking and kissing began again until they both lay quietly listening to the cats assaulting the door, indignant that they had been shut out.

That weekend, Jessie made another trip to the doctor and was taken off the crutches and out of the brace and given some physical therapy and exercises to do. When she returned to work mid-week, still limping, things seemed pretty quiet. Georgia's office, just beyond hers, was locked and minus the usual activity of students coming by to see her. The hallway was even quieter now. Sarah had greeted her warmly with some sympathy for her knee and given her the messages and work that had piled up while she'd been gone.

At lunch Jessie limped over to the student union. Burford was so small that faculty mostly grouped around a couple of tables at lunch time, coming and going as their schedules allowed. Lucy moved over to make room for her.

"How's the knee?" she asked.

"It's better. It was in a brace, but they said if I do the exercises they gave me, that should strengthen it," Jessie answered.

Lucy sighed, looking around the table. "It's just not the same without Georgia. She'd been gone on her two-year research leave, and we'd just gotten her back. It was so nice to have someone to talk to again."

"She seemed to have many friends," Jessie offered.

"Yes, Georgia was generally the one in the know.

It irked her that she wasn't here when Joyce Barnette went through her troubles. They always spent a lot of time together. Hard to believe that they're both dead," Lucy said, beginning to gather her tray.

Jessie realized that Georgia had accompanied Joyce to most of the Burford events since her return; in fact, Georgia had been the only woman faculty member Jessie had seen with Joyce. "Do you really think that Georgia's death was accident?" Jessie asked. "She wanted to tell me something about Joyce's death that day. It's just too convenient. Had she said anything to you?"

Before Lucy could answer, Chris came in in her usual Army-green raincoat and purple bookbag. She pulled a chair over to the group, took off her coat and threw her things on the chair. Jessie noticed something shining on the bookbag. When she looked closer, she saw it was a tiny pink triangle pin like the one Georgia had worn. A chill went through her. She remembered the rip on Georgia's sweater where the pin would have been.

"Are you feeling all right, Jessie? You look pale," Chris asked when she saw her looking at it. She gave her a little smirk and before Jessie could say anything, she went to get her lunch.

Jessie didn't know what to think, but she had to leave to go teach her class.

As she walked across the quad to her office, she thought about the fact that Georgia had seemed to be Joyce's only friend, and now this appearance of the triangle pin. She was sure that Georgia's death hadn't been an accident, but of course, she had no proof. She hadn't seen Chris anywhere near the area, although she remembered seeing Pam riding back toward the village.

Whoever had done it could have left the path the way Jessie had when she went for help. She wondered how someone could have gotten Georgia off the path and down the embankment on her bike. To kill her would have required that the bike went off the path at full speed. So the element of surprise would have been necessary. Maybe the killer injured her first and pushed her over the side. On a bike going down the hill, Georgia would have had much less control than if she fell climbing down as Jessie had. She wondered if there had been any unusual marks on her body that might suggest that she was injured before going over. She hadn't noticed any, but she hadn't been looking. She guessed that if the police had found any or any suggestion of obstacles placed on the path, they wouldn't have ruled it an accident. This time whoever did it was more clever than whoever killed Joyce. She hadn't been back to the area since she'd found Georgia, but she was certain that it was messed up so much by now that there would be nothing left to find. But that triangle pin on Chris's bag! Did what Georgia want to tell her have something to do with Joyce's murder? Who would have wanted Georgia dead?

The horror of finding Georgia Swain's mangled and lifeless body lying at the bottom of the embankment came back to her. By the time she got to the classroom, she was shaking and tears were beginning to come unbidden. She had to pause outside the classroom to try and calm herself and force the tears to stop. She felt that once they got started, the terror of the last few weeks would rush out in a torrent and she would be unable to quit. She didn't want to give in to her emotions and break down in front of her students, but she was very close to doing so. For a daughter of the military, this would be shameful.

She lost the battle. Tears started streaming silently down her cheeks. Embarrassed, she went over to where her teaching assistants sat.

"Joan, would you run the video?" she asked, trying to ignore the tears.

Joan nodded and Jessie could see the concern in her eyes.

Jessie picked up the video which she noted ironically was *Pink Triangles* and handed it to Jennifer.

"I'm going home. I'm not feeling well and I'm going home," she said, reaching into her briefcase for a Kleenex.

"Go ahead and break up into discussion groups as usual after the video. I'll see you next week." Jessie sniffed.

"Do you want us to collect the student papers and leave them with Sarah?" one of the other T.A.s asked.

"That would be very helpful," Jessie answered. She turned and left the room. She could feel the eyes of her students on her. She went straight to the elevator, hoping no one would be in it. The tears coursed quietly down her face. She walked quickly by the glassed-in room where her secretary usually sat, but the room was empty. She could see the light streaming into the dim hall from Chris's office.

As she got closer to Chris's office, the tears came

harder and the shaking began again. She was terrified that she would run into her. Chris seemed to be growing ever more malevolent in her mind. Had she actually sneered at her in the cafeteria? She made herself walk past Chris's office to her own door without looking in. She inserted the key in her lock, opened the door and pushed it shut behind her, the tears still flowing and her nose running. She grabbed another tissue and blew her nose, willing the tears to quit. She tried to be quiet; the walls were thin and she didn't want Chris to hear. It was a point of honor. You didn't let the enemy know they had gotten to you. She wasn't quite sure if Chris had become an enemy, but she knew that she couldn't trust her.

She grabbed her coat and her briefcase and pulled the large brim of her felt hat down over her eyes. She quietly left her office and went out the back way so as not to pass Chris's office again and headed down the hill, her tears half-blinding her.

Once inside her small house, the calico cat greeted her, standing on the armchair near the door and yowling. Throwing her things onto the chair, Jessie grabbed the cat, holding her to her face and convulsively sobbing into the soft fur. The cat, never liking to be confined, pulled away, jumped from her arms and retreated. Jessie was left with a face full of fur. She went into the bathroom to wash her face. The other cat and the kitten watched as Jessie came out and collapsed onto the couch.

Several hours later when Lynn came home, Jessie still lay on the couch. She had fallen asleep, exhausted after making some notes on the cases in her notebook. The kitten lay sprawled across her lap.

The calico had draped herself on the back of the couch and the gray rested at her feet.

Lynn looked at her and said, "What happened?"

"I'm not really sure," she said, sitting up and scattering the cats. "I saw a pink triangle on Chris Stendal's bookbag at lunch, and it seemed to trigger everything from the past few weeks. Georgia —" She stopped, starting to cry again.

Lynn put down her briefcase and sat on the couch. She pulled Jessie to her and held her. When the sobbing subsided she handed her a tissue and said, "Did Chris say something to you?"

Jessie blew her nose and said, "Just that I looked pale, but I could have sworn she sneered at me. Oh, Lynn, do you think she had Georgia's triangle pin? It's like she's flaunting it, daring me to try to do something about it. Does that mean she murdered Georgia?"

"There's probably no way to prove it's Georgia's pin. You never saw Chris have a pin like that before?" she asked, smoothing back Jessie's hair from her face. "I think *I* have a pin like that somewhere."

"I guess I'm just oversensitive because of seeing Georgia have one like it and then her sweater being torn where it would have been. I seem to be seeing triangle pins everywhere now. I don't feel like I want to see Chris again, much less have an office next to hers. Something about her scares me, and I don't want to fall apart every time I see her."

"Maybe she won't have that effect next time you see her," Lynn said thoughtfully. "She could have just triggered emotions you bottled up — from Joyce's death and from the stress of being in a new place. Just a minute."

Lynn got up and left the room. When she came back, she had a small carved stone goddess on a length of cording. "I was saving this for your birthday, but I think you could use it now. Keep her with you and use her to center yourself when you need to."

Jessie took the figure, feeling its cool, smooth curves. "Oh, she's a Venus of Willendorf! Thank you; she's beautiful." She slipped the cord over her head and tucked it into her shirt to rest between her breasts. "I feel better already."

CHAPTER 9

The next week Jessie tried going to work again. When she got there with the tiny stone goddess resting in its hidden spot, she didn't have time to worry about whether she would run into Chris Stendal or not. Chris seemed to be waiting for her.

"Oh Jessie, I wanted to show you this before anyone else did," she said brightly. "Have you seen *The Chronicle of Higher Education* — the Quotable Comments section?"

"No, I can't say that I have. Why?" Jessie replied coolly, wondering what Chris was up to.

"A sentence from one of your memos is featured. See, this typo makes it really funny- — 'The Women's Studies Program can offer *pubic* forums,' " she said, showing Jessie the piece. Jessie frowned, and Chris said, "Oh sorry, I didn't mean to upset you — just thought you'd want to know," and she went into her office.

Jessie was left fuming, the goddess forgotten. "This takes the cake," she muttered. Who would do such a mean-spirited thing — to make women's studies and her look foolish on a national level! "Just lovely!"

Later, she thought Chris seemed too pleased about it. She might have sent it in herself. It was becoming more and more apparent that Jessie's sense that they were enemies was real, but she didn't know how it had happened. She couldn't remember anything she might have done to offend her, and she believed that she must have done something to cause rupture between them. It was hard for her to accept that they could be both enemies and feminists. Weren't they working for the same things? Shouldn't that transcend any difficulties between them? It seemed especially hard because she was also a lesbian, and Jessie considered lesbians, especially lesbian-feminists, as family. They were her chosen family, after all. Her biological family had rejected her not long after she and Lynn had gotten together some fourteen years ago. She hadn't expected "instant" family when she came here, but as a group the lesbians had been so nice that she'd been taken off guard and believed the accepting face they'd shown her.

She had known that she might have some difficulty with Chris. From her experience of moving around with her father's frequent transfers, she was familiar with the jealousy that could arise toward the new kid. For lack of other faculty, Chris had been holding the Women's Center and Women's Studies together — but as an administrator, not on tenure track. Her territory, however, was thoroughly established. She had acted as if she was happy to give over the Women's Studies area to Jessie, saying she had too much work to do, but it was becoming clear that Chris coveted the tenure-track Women's Studies position. During the first few months, Jessie had gone out of her way to consult her, hoping to make the younger woman feel appreciated, and she had really needed her help to get used to Burford. Now she was distant and Jessie didn't know what had gone wrong.

Pulling out the goddess from her resting place, Jessie held it in her hand for a moment, gathering up her courage. Then she went to Chris's office.

The door was open and Jessie rapped on the frame. "Can I come in?"

Chris was sitting at the computer in front of the window at the back of the narrow space. At Jessie's knock, she turned in her swivel chair and nodded. Wearing a yellow sweater with olive green pants, her hair shining in the sunlight, she looked thinner than Jessie had remembered. There were tired circles under her eyes.

"I was wondering," Jessie began a little nervously, "if there's some problem between us. You seem so distant. Have I done something to offend you?"

"No, I'm just tired. I've been up all night, too — moving into our other bedroom. Pam and I are splitting up."

"Splitting up? I'm sorry — that's really hard. How long have you been together?" Jessie was surprised.

"Five years," Chris said with a sigh. "We're going to try just sharing the house for a while. Pam can't stay in faculty housing without me, and she's got golf tournaments coming up. And I've got too much going on here. Frankly, I can't afford to move out right now. Despite all this mayhem at Burford, I'm defending my dissertation next week. I'm reworking a piece of it for publication in *Women's Studies International* right now. It's past due. And with all this other stuff..." She gestured at the piles littering her office.

"Well, congratulations on finishing! Will you go through graduation?"

"Yes, I think I'll do a job search, too. I don't think I want to stay in a non-tenure track position now that I have my Ph.D. and things are so uncertain with Pam. Did you see my new gown?" She got up and unzipped a black bag hanging on the coat rack behind the door. Inside was a black academic gown and hood, and to Jessie's admiring glances she drew out a tam-style academic hat instead of the old mortar board. "I ordered it through Burford. You know we wear our gowns here at least three times a year — once for the parents and new students at freshman installation in the fall, once for honors convocation in the spring and again for graduation. Most of the faculty have their own gowns."

Jessie nodded. "Yes, I have my own hood, but I had to borrow a plain robe and one of their awful mortarboards from the bookstore last fall. What a nice shape," she said, examining Chris's tam. "You wouldn't have to worry about it being on crooked.

Well, congratulations again, and let me know if there's anything I can do to help you and Pam," she said, somewhat relieved.

"Please don't tell anyone. After a public commitment ceremony a year ago, this is pretty embarrassing," she said.

As Chris brushed back her bangs, Jessie could see a large bruise on her forehead. She started to say something, but thought better of it, just nodded her acquiescence and went back to her office.

Jessie wanted to believe that there were no problems between them. Certainly, there was much going on in Chris's life that would account for her distance. Jessie would be up for her mid-year evaluation sooner than seemed possible, and she would need a letter from Chris. Since there was no one else officially assigned to the Women's Studies Program except Jessie, it was difficult to figure out who would evaluate her. She supposed they would put together some sort of committee to take the place of the colleagues she didn't officially have. In any case, she knew Chris would be important to her contract renewal.

Jessie had been surprised at the pomp Burford put on. She had never been anywhere that academic gowns were used for more than graduation. She was also skeptical about Chris's job search. If Chris didn't intend to stay at Burford, why would she spend the money for a gown to be worn as infrequently as most universities do? If she had said that she bought it because she was so excited about finishing her Ph.D., not an easy task while holding down a full-time position, that would make more sense. Maybe with this latest development with Pam, leaving was a more recent idea. Jessie wondered about the bruise. She supposed that Chris could have gotten the bruise moving stuff around last night. Jessie sensed something hostile about Pam Effelton, though. Chris had hinted once before about a problem between them that she didn't want to talk about. Had Pam hit her or pushed her down?

Jessie reached for the little goddess and tried to put her worries about what was going on with Chris and her own impending renewal evaluation out of her mind. She concentrated on rubbing the stone.

Jessie called the Women's Studies Committee together later that week to discuss the problem with Lucy's department and the idea that she should teach their introductory course. She had decided to face the problem head-on, but since Lucy was on the Women's Studies Committee, she knew it was going to be an awkward meeting. Jessie had had some success in a previous administrative position with mediating between two staff members, but of course, she wasn't in the middle of it then. She had been awake for hours in the middle of the night, mentally running through what to say.

"I don't like what is happening with my affiliation," Jessie explained as tactfully as she could, watching Lucy tap her Birkenstocks. "It feels like a way of controlling the Women's Studies director position. My contract clearly says that I'm in Women's Studies despite any affiliation. What if I unaffiliate?" Jessie paused.

Carmel Gratio shook her dark curls. "It isn't right. I don't think we can let this happen."

Denise Oberon nodded in agreement. "Yes, this never would have happened if I'd continued as director."

"Well, of course not," Carmel said in exasperation. "You're a tenured full professor. Nobody would tell you what you had to teach."

"Since I'm not a faculty member, I don't know what I can do," Chris said, reminding everyone of her status as an administrator.

Lucy continued to sit there without saying anything. Carmel turned to her and said, "Lucy, can't you, Denise and Jessie write up a request to the dean that Jessie's assignment be changed to just Women's Studies?"

Lucy nodded and said gruffly, "What do you want me to say?

Jessie was happy to see Christmas break come around. The last month had flown by, and she'd spent Thanksgiving weekend reading papers while Lynn went along to visit her family. Jessie didn't mind. She much preferred December's festivities. She and Lynn planned a Solstice party for the local lesbian community. Quite a number lived in the area, and Lynn had gotten to know them through a social group for older lesbians. When Jessie had arrived on campus, she met Betty Jasper who worked in the central office, who thereafter served as Lynn and Jessie's staff connection to what was happening on

71

campus and to the local community. Betty was the first to arrive.

"Hello, Betty, come in," Lynn said, pulling the door open wide. "Let me take your coat."

Betty handed Lynn her jacket and stood looking around at the decorations. "The house looks wonderful," she said.

"Yes, Jessie likes the holidays, especially the lights. Speaking of lights, would you believe that we actually got a notice from the neighborhood that we should put electric candles in our front windows and where to buy them? Not much thought given to diversity in this neighborhood. I can't wait to move out of here!" Lynn said with feeling.

"Oh hi, Betty. Is she ranting about the elitism in the neighborhood again? It's one of her pet peeves," Jessie said. "Come on, Lynn. This is supposed to be a party. I just got off the phone with Denise. She and Jennifer aren't coming, and I gather most of the other faculty aren't either. It seems that tonight they planned a big party to celebrate Jennifer's birthday. She tried to get me to have ours another night, but she didn't invite us to hers. I told her we'd have another party. I hope there won't be more trouble from this."

Betty sat down on the couch and said, "Well, I'm not surprised. Most of the faculty don't mingle with the local lesbians, anyway. You notice that none of them ever come to our social events. Most of them aren't very nice to me, either, particularly Chris Stendal. They certainly never acknowledge me." She sighed. "I miss Joyce. She was one of the few who were friendly. We used to have lunch once in a while. Then all that business with Chris and now she's gone."

"Yes, Burford *is* quite a place. The lesbians seem particularly fractionalized, but I think Chris and Pam are coming over. She seemed upset that she wasn't invited to Denise's party. I hope her being here won't be a problem for you," Jessie said. "I didn't know you were a friend of Joyce's."

"Don't worry about it. Chris can be a very good politician. I'm sure she'll be on her best behavior. Weren't you having problems with her?"

"Well, she seemed distant for a while, but I talked to her. I guess she just had a lot on her mind."

"Well, watch your back," Betty said. "She's a climber. She'll do anything to enhance her reputation. She'll have your position if she can."

"You know, I still haven't found out who put the threatening flyer on my car up on campus, even though I reported it to security."

"You reported it to Bob Martin?" Betty said, laughing. She took a Christmas cookie from the plate on the coffee table.

"Yes, what's so funny?" Jessie asked.

"He has a reputation for burying any complaint. Burford loves him. Any case you take to him never sees the light of day. Did he say he'd show it to the local police?" Betty asked.

"Yes, he did." Jessie said, frowning.

"Did they ever contact you about it?"

"No, they didn't."

"Exactly my point," Betty said. "He's particularly unsympathetic to complaints from female faculty and

73

students. One spring we had a flasher exposing himself to some of the women, and Bob wanted to know what they'd done to encourage him. Had they gone around scantily dressed? He's a dinosaur. Don't expect much from him."

"Betty, what can I get you to drink?" Lynn asked. We have mulled cider, spring water, coffee, or wine."

"I'll try the cider. These cookies are good," she said, taking another. "And what a gorgeous tree. Are those bubble lights? We used to have those when I was a kid."

"Yes, I did too. These are new ones, though. I was so pleased when I found them. Trees are actually a pagan ritual, so they fit in with a Solstice celebration," Jessie said.

Coming back with the cider, Lynn said, "I see that you and I are going to be on the same task force to plan the local police-training for domestic violence. I hope they're better than Burford's security officers."

The doorbell rang and Jessie got up to let in Chris and Pam and several of the local lesbians. When Chris and Pam had settled with their drinks, Chris said, "Are we the only ones from Burford?" eyeing Betty with some surprise and a fleeting moment of distaste.

"Denise is having a party for Jennifer. I guess most of them are there. She asked me to change the night of our party but made it clear that we wouldn't be invited — only Jennifer's *good* friends are," Jessie said.

"Why, you're a good friend, aren't you, Chris? There must have been some mistake," Pam said defensively.

Chris frowned sightly, but didn't say anything. To break the silence Jessie said, "I like your pants, Pam. Wool, aren't they?" Pam was wearing a pair of beautiful pale cream pants.

"Thanks. Chris tells me you always look great. I wish she could take some pointers from you. We're trying to update her image," Pam said.

Jessie shrugged. "Well, I've had years of teaching to accumulate a wardrobe. I taught before I got my Ph.D."

Later, Jessie thought maybe she shouldn't have been so quick to agree with Pam about Chris's way of dressing. Chris hadn't seemed very friendly after that conversation. Despite all her efforts, Jessie didn't feel she was doing very well juggling the political demands of her position.

CHAPTER 10

Just after the new semester began, Jessie came to work one morning before Sarah had arrived. The hall was dark — no one had switched on the lights to counter the dim winter morning, and all the office doors were shut. Jessie flipped the light switch on but it didn't alter the melancholy feeling in the hall. She supposed Burford was saving on electricity. Early morning classes were rare at Burford. Most of the students preferred to sleep in, especially after the rowdy weekend parties. She could hear nothing in the big, old building. When she passed Chris's door, she saw that someone had defaced the door with graffiti — drawings of penises and the words *whore* and *cunt*. Jessie's door had more penises and *bitch* and *cocksucker* scrawled on her door.

Jessie unlocked her door and took off her coat. She started to reach for the telephone when she heard a noise in the hall. Startled, she whirled around. Sarah appeared in the doorway.

"Sorry if I scared you. I see we've been visited by a graffiti artist." She sighed. "I'll call security," she said, poking at a penis with a finger. "This doesn't look like it will come off easily. I'll notify the janitor to bring his cleaning supplies."

"Has this happened much in the past?" Jessie asked.

"I haven't seen anything as crude as this. A few years back, Georgia Swain had *liberal* and *bleeding heart* written on her office door, but students seem to have gotten bolder. I'll go call now."

A half-hour passed before Bob Martin from security appeared in her doorway. "Your secretary called about this," he said, examining a penis as if it were a signed work of art. "Have you been having difficulty with a student?" he asked puffing, himself up and talking in an unnaturally husky voice.

"No, I haven't even given many grades yet," Jessie replied. "I've been meaning to ask you, did you make any progress on who put that threatening flyer on my windshield or, for that matter, who put out the flyer in the first place?"

Bob adjusted his hat with the word *Security* on the front and looked boldly into her eyes. "We have a

77

few leads. I'll let you know when we know something for sure." He turned and walked out of the room with a sort of swagger.

Later, Jessie found out from Sarah that one of the fraternity boys had had penile drawings on his room door as decoration and Bob had recognized the style and confronted him. Jessie supposed it was a "boys will be boys" kind of confrontation — not even important enough for Bob to inform her personally or divulge the name of the perpetrator. Sarah said it wasn't anyone she or Chris had had in class, but Jessie felt that since their doors had been singled out, it added to the hostile environment. She was surprised that the graffiti had said nothing about their being lesbians — it was just general anti-woman sentiment.

Jessie got her evaluations back from first semester, and they were not good. In fact, in her fifteen years of teaching, she had seldom had such poor evaluations. Of course, she'd never had to teach women's studies as a requirement to such a reluctant group. Next year she'd do some work to see if she couldn't attract more interested students. A hangover from the old idealist period in women's studies, the course was pass or fail — the only one that met the minority studies requirement at Burford to be ungraded. Her sections were full of fraternity and sorority juniors and seniors who took them as an easy way out. That way, they figured, they wouldn't have to work very hard and they wouldn't have to confront racism by taking a black studies course.

They didn't know that women's studies concerned racism, heterosexism and a host of other "isms" too. No wonder that the evaluations were poor. She had never seen so many young women convinced that the bad old days were gone and that women had it made. She was really the bearer of bad tidings and the inclination was "to kill the messenger," she feared.

Jessie had heard that Chris's evaluations weren't much better for a similar class, and other new faculty had complained about their women's studies evaluations, too. But still, it was a shock to Jessie. She thought making it a graded course might eventually change its population, and she might even attract some students who would like to major or minor in women's studies. The major and minor was really a joke, something that Burford used for publicity. Mostly women's studies courses were service courses, meeting a requirement for students to graduate with no actual majors and few minors.

The students who showed real interest in women's studies were attending on scholarship and had some idea of what faced them outside Burford. They were her prized students — all two of them. Jessie wondered if she'd be given a chance to change the class, though. She realized that these evaluations would be the ones looked at for renewal. It didn't look good, she thought, reaching for the little goddess.

Despite Chris's revelation that she and Pam were splitting up, Jessie saw them together frequently. They had seemed okay at the Solstice party, although a tension had been present that Jessie couldn't quite put her finger on. Often Pam would bring the dog up to Chris's office in the afternoons to visit. One day after Pam and the dog left, Jessie went into Chris's office. "You all seem pretty chummy these days. Have you made up?"

Chris looked up from her paperwork. "Yes, we're getting along fine now. Thanks for asking."

"The dog certainly has grown. She seems pretty well behaved when she comes to your office," Jessie said for lack of something else to say.

Chris brightened and said, "Yes, Pam's been taking her to obedience lessons. She's the only one who can manage her. I haven't had time to go, but I'd like to learn how to make her mind. Has she been in your flower beds again?"

"No, not for a while. I know you try to keep her in your yard," Jessie said. "I see Pam walking her on a leash a lot."

"Well, sometimes she gets away. She really likes to chase cats. Pulled away from Pam entirely the other night. We're hoping that the obedience lessons will help."

"We never let the cats out. You don't have to worry about them." She paused. "This hall certainly is quiet without Georgia. I know that they moved some of the computers into that office for the math faculty, but I never see anyone using them."

They chatted for a few more minutes, then Jessie left, still disturbed by Chris's distance.

CHAPTER 11

In late January just before her evaluation, Jessie realized that because she had taken credit for several years of college work before coming to Burford, she would be evaluated as if she had been Director of Women's Studies for four years instead of just one. In February, she gathered all of her courage to meet with the dean, even taking along some sympathetic faculty to try to convince the administration to give her a first-year review instead of a fourth-year review. The evaluation process had changed in the last few years and even the older faculty hadn't known what advice to give her about taking credit for previous teaching. Without a union, there were no safeguards on how the administration shaped the process. Eventually, the faculty would catch on and might organize to rebel, but it would be too late for Jessie and others caught in the whims of the administration.

The morning Jessie was to meet with the dean, her old fear of male authority had risen full-force, and she found herself shaking when she went out to get into the car. She was late and decided to drive up the hill to save time. When she turned the key in the ignition, nothing happened — not a sound. She tried again — nothing. With no time to figure out what was wrong, she grabbed her briefcase and began the long climb up the hill at a run which soon slowed to a fast trot. By the time she reached the meeting, out of breath and panting, everyone was assembled around the big polished table in the crowded conference room, waiting for her.

"Oh, Jessie, I thought you'd decided not to come," Lucy Taft said when Jessie came in and slid into the vacant chair.

"Sorry, I had car trouble," Jessie said, knowing that the excuse sounded ridiculous since she just lived at the bottom of the hill.

Dean Whiffle, dressed in his dark suit and tie, nodded to Jessie to begin.

"I wanted to meet with you," she explained, "because I'd like to be evaluated as a first-year director instead of a fourth-year director. When I took the credit for previous teaching experience, I thought it had to do with salary, not the review cycle. This system is unlike any I've experienced."

"Well, I will have to take this to the college's review committee. I'll let you know," he said, looking at her with a little smile.

Jessie nodded and the meeting was over without further discussion. She realized that all her worry about this meeting was for nothing; it had been brief and the dean had made no decision. She might as well not had it. She could have just written her request instead of anguishing over a meeting.

The night before she had slept badly. She had woken up with hot flashes, and then anxious thoughts kept her awake for hours. This pattern had begun to happen frequently. Lynn had been the opposite. She had started the menopause process early and had had plenty of hot flashes, but she just seemed to sleep all the time when she wasn't working.

Jessie thanked her supporters for coming, especially Lucy Taft, who was on the college committee. At least, she thought, she'd have someone on the committee to explain her case — that as a new faculty member and the only one in her program, she'd had no one to advise her about taking previous credit. But then she remembered that Lucy wasn't exactly a supporter. She had hardly spoken to Jessie since she had unaffiliated with Lucy's department.

As she walked back across the quad to her office she thought about her options. She knew that the year before, a female faculty member had won a settlement when she lost her position after an early fourth-year review. If the review committee denied her petition for a first-year review, and the fourth-year review went badly, she could contact the same lawyer.

She wondered what was wrong with her car. It had always started before. She wondered if it was the ignition. When she reached her office, she decided to call home. Lynn was taking the morning off and might be there now, finished with her errands.

Jessie unlocked the door to her office, deposited her briefcase and took off her coat. At her desk, she dialed home. Finally, Lynn answered.

"Lynn, I'm glad you're there," she said with relief.

"I just walked in. What happened at your meeting with the dean?"

"You won't believe the morning I've had." Jessie sighed. "I was late so I decided to take the car, but when I tried to start it, nothing happened — not a sound. Would you take a look at it and call me back? Anyway, I had to run up the hill — came crashing into the meeting late. The meeting lasted about two minutes. Dean Whiffle said it would have to go the college committee. But Lucy's on the committee so it may be all right or it may not be, if she's holding a grudge about my affiliation. If it isn't, I think I'll call that lawyer we were told about."

"Doesn't sound like the meeting was worth all the effort. I noticed that you had another anxiety attack last night. You were up for hours. Can you come home early?" Lynn asked, sounding concerned.

"Not until after class."

"So something's wrong with your car? Sure, I'll take a look at it and call you back."

Jessie hung up and a few minutes later, the phone rang.

"Jessie?" Lynn was chuckling.

"Lynn, what's so funny?" Jessie asked.

"I found out why your car won't start," Lynn said. "It doesn't have a battery or any gas."

"What? No battery? No gas? You mean someone took the battery out and siphoned my gas right there in plain view of the street?" Jessie was incredulous.

"Apparently so."

"What next?" Jessie asked.

Later that week, Lucy stopped by Jessie's office. Jessie had never seen her in anything but Birkenstocks, and she wasn't disappointed this time.

"Jessie, I just stopped in to tell you that the college committee met. You'll probably get your letter from the dean today. They wouldn't let me say anything at the meeting — said it would prejudice the case. The dean wouldn't identify you, and the boys on the committee kept saying things like, 'Wouldn't the faculty member's department chair have told him?' They ruled against you. Sorry, I've done all I can. You can write a letter of protest to the dean."

"Thanks anyway," Jessie said frowning. "You did what you could," she said out loud, but she didn't believe it.

That evening, as Jessie was out looking at her tulips and daffodils beginning to push though the earth, Lynn drove up. "Look at this," she said as Lynn came up the walk. "Chris and Pam's Doberman has been over here again digging." She pointed to a small pile of torn tulip leaves. "That dog has gotten huge. It's no wonder they can't control it. Of course, Pam *had* to have a purebred."

Jessie followed Lynn inside, then gave her a hug. "Let's just leave this place now and go somewhere else — admit it was a terrible mistake. This is one time that I wish I was still in the military and we could just be given another assignment. Like when I was in the seventh grade and things started turning sour. It was okay because I knew my dad was due for a transfer and we'd be leaving soon."

Lynn pulled back a little and said, "Now what happened?"

"Oh, I received a formal letter from the dean saying that my petition has been denied.. They will continue with the fourth-year review. And guess who he appointed to chair my committee? Denise. She was so vicious to Carrie Small, the only other lesbian-feminist in her department. When Carrie came up for tenure, she cast the tie-breaking vote against her tenure."

"Oh, great! So now Chris's warnings about 'watch out for Denise' can come true," Lynn said. "Well, we've survived other things this bad. We'll get through this, too."

"Well, Denise was the chair of my search committee, and I have been working pretty closely with her, so maybe it'll work out. She's been Acting Director of Women's Studies in the past. She certainly knows what the position entails. She also prides herself on getting the last Women's Studies Director through the tenure process." Jessie slumped down on the couch.

"Ah, more military optimism, hmm?"

"Maybe I should think about getting out of academia," Jessie said, saddened by the thought. "I just don't know if I can go through another national search for a position — after all those one- and two-year positions. Moving again to another job, even if I find one, and starting this all over again."

Lynn came over and pulled her close, smoothing her hair. "Don't think about that now. Even if it doesn't go well, you have another year here. We'll have time to think what to do. Maybe we should take my mother up on her offer of letting us live in the cabin in Idaho."

"Oh, right! And do what?" Jessie said, pulling away angrily.

"Okay, I can see that won't be one of the options," Lynn said soothingly.

Despite Lynn's reassurances that everything would be all right, Jessie knew that the strain of the situation was taking a toll on Lynn. She still hadn't recovered from moving and her blood pressure was often high, leaving her disoriented. One night Jessie had come home to find Lynn sitting despondent at the dining room table. When Lynn saw Jessie, she started crying.

"Where have you been? I was so worried. I thought something had happened to you," she said, her voice muffled between sobs.

Jessie knew this was serious. Lynn rarely cried. She usually put on a front to cover her feelings.

"Lynn, did you forget? I told you I was going

over to Carmel Gratio's. She was having an informal get-together. She just lives a few blocks from here. You could have come."

"I couldn't remember her last name or address. I tried to call the Burford operator to see if they knew where you were . . ." Lynn's voice trailed off.

"It's okay. I'm fine. I'm here now," Jessie said.

Lynn wasn't making sense, but Jessie knew that when Lynn's blood pressure was up, there wasn't much she could do except try to reassure her. She wasn't her usual logical, self-sufficient self when this was happening. These spells were coming often, and Jessie was worried. When Lynn was thinking more clearly, she'd have to talk to her about going to the doctor.

CHAPTER 12

In a fourth-year review, Jessie was to have letters from students and faculty. Jessie gave Denise a list of students, but since she'd been at Burford such a short time, the list was brief. It included some of her best students from her previous position, but she wondered if Burford would even take any information from the outside seriously since these were state university students. Burford was insistent on indulging its particular clientele of wealthy students. The state university students who would write for her were older, more mature, with some experience of the world. By and large, they knew about racism and sexism and had taken her classes as electives.

Then, too, she was reticent to brag about herself. In the military world she grew up in, you followed the rules, did a good job, and your superior evaluated your performance. Her mother's admonition, "Don't blow your own horn," kept coming back to her. She found the evaluation process embarrassing.

About halfway through the process at the end of February, Jessie became nervous, wondering if she had any letters from the Women's Studies faculty. If she had been in a real department instead of a program of one, her colleagues would have been required to write letters. But in this case, it was voluntary, and so many of the faculty were untenured. One day she even nervously asked Chris Stendal if she had written a letter. Chris had looked up from the pile on her desk and said, "Of course." Somehow that didn't make Jessie feel any better, but she kept trying to believe in Chris's good will.

Jessie saw Denise one morning and asked about the letters. "Oh hi, Jessie," Denise said. "Letters? You mean for your review. Yes, some are coming in. I've been meaning to tell you that your last class evaluations are good. You should be pleased. The committee is going to meet soon to evaluate your materials. I've got to go to class. Talk to you later," and she rushed out the door onto the quad, leaving Jessie feeling breathless.

Finally, her committee met to look over her materials. She saw Denise in the hall one Friday afternoon, and Denise said, "If you're worried about our recommending you for renewal, don't give it a moment's thought. I'll meet with you Monday to tell you about our decision."

Jessie went home hoping that things were going to turn out all right — maybe Denise's persecution of Carrie was not a pattern, but just a fluke. Then Jessie remembered the hurt look in Denise's eyes when she talked about being Acting Women's Studies Director. Denise hadn't been asked to do it again. Would that somehow boomerang on her? And what part would Lucy Taft play on the committee?

Despite her lingering misgivings, Jessie went home somewhat relieved, determined to enjoy the weekend. She was feeling fairly good and decided to weed the lawn. She enjoyed doing things with her hands after all the brain work of academia, even though she didn't really care much about whether the lawn, which was just starting to green up, had weeds in it. The hill in front of their house was so steep that Jessie could stand on the sidewalk and pull weeds from the lower part of the lawn without bending over. If it hadn't been a rented house, they would have put in ground cover. The lawn was a devil to mow, and they'd borrowed Chris and Pam's mower until they'd gotten one of their own.

Betty came down the sidewalk on her way home. "It's looking good," she said, indicating the yard. Looks like you're going to have some nice tulips. Did you plant those?"

"Yes, last fall. This yard didn't have much in the way of plants," Jessie said. "If we move, we thought we could always dig them up and take them with us. I hear even if you get tenure they make you move."

"Yes, that's the tradition. You only get faculty housing while you have a temporary position," Betty said, nodding. "I heard the residence management people talking about what a nice job you two had done with this place. They said they wished all the faculty did such a nice job." Betty glanced toward Pam and Chris's overgrown garden which hadn't been cleaned out for spring. "Would you like to borrow my weedcutter for the weeds in the rocks? Actually, I'll come and cut them myself, if you like. I enjoy using it — something satisfying in whipping those weeds." She laughed.

Lynn pulled her car up to the curb, got out and came over to Jessie and Betty. "Hi, Betty," she said putting her briefcase and a brown bag down on the sidewalk. "Happy Friday!" To Jessie she said, "You look chipper. Any news?"

"Well, Denise assures me that they're going to recommend me for renewal. I'm meeting with her on Monday to get the official word," Jessie said happily.

"Good," Lynn said. "I brought home champagne — figured we'd celebrate life changes no matter what. Want to come in for a while, Betty?"

"Nope, got to get home. Thanks anyway. Glad to hear that the committee is doing the right thing." Betty gave a little wave and was off.

"I've got more stuff in the car. Help me, will you?" Lynn opened the trunk.

"Sure," Jessie said, taking the proffered bag. "What do you have in here?"

"I picked up some Chinese. Thought we'd have dinner in and maybe a romantic evening. You've been sleeping so poorly, I'm hoping that I can make you forget about work."

"Sounds delightful," Jessie said, following Lynn into the house.

On Monday, after the Women's Studies meeting, Jessie followed Denise into her office and sat down in a chair next to her desk. Denise had on her casual but preppy sweater and slacks in the usual pale colors that accented her light brown hair. Jessie watched nervously as Denise picked up a folder from her desk and took out the notes the committee had made. Denise's voice didn't even waver when she said, "Instead of a direct contract renewal, we recommended you for probation. If the administration agrees, you would be reviewed again next year for a two-year contract renewal before being considered for tenure. A few of the letters showed that you alienated some of the people with whom you work, and others said you needed to be more of a visible presence on campus — speak out, for instance, at a faculty meeting."

Jessie was so taken aback after the assurance which Denise had given her earlier that she hardly knew what to say. She sat there stunned, barely hearing Denise's comments. Her heart was racing, and there was a buzz in her ears.

Denise continued, "The college review committee will decide what you need to do to improve as director if they give you another year beyond next year. However, the college committee doesn't like giving probation; it usually doesn't work out, so I'm

93

writing to try to convince them. Your record of publishing is excellent, and your teaching has improved. We are going to *try* to keep you."

"Try? But you aren't recommending that my contract be renewed?" Jessie gasped.

When she had recovered from the shock of Denise's pronouncement, she tried not to argue with her, not to appear defensive. She didn't want to let her know how betrayed she felt. She needed to get out of there to think about what had happened before she responded — to let this latest turn of events sink in. Denise had prepared a list of things Jessie could do to improve, and the one small thing that Jessie did ask was that the list not be sent with the recommendation for probation. The list made it look as though the committee really believed every negative thing anyone had said in a letter. And it later dawned on her that of course, they did.

Jessie left the meeting feeling sick. Her first thought was that somehow her secretary had been unhappy with her. She went to Sarah first. "I just had my review meeting with Denise, and she said that I had alienated those with whom I was working closest. Have you and I had some difficulties that I should know about?"

Sarah looked embarrassed as she said, "No, it wasn't me. I haven't been complaining about you."

Sarah looked down at her desk and said something about Chris, but Jessie was in such a state, and the situation was so awkward that she hadn't really heard and didn't want to ask again. She left Sarah's office for her own. She reached for the little goddess nestled between her breasts, but no amount of rubbing the smooth stone would soothe her.

Jessie went to teach her class. She had a guest speaker and didn't have to do much but be there. The speaker was a counselor from Burford's student center talking about eating disorders among the college population. As Jessie sat there dejectedly, she thought, "yes, that's a disease that women are particularly prone to. She, for one, didn't care if she ever ate again."

She was so depressed that she hadn't noticed that the speaker had stopped and was looking at her for a signal to end the class. Jessie tried to pull herself together and told the class in a flat voice that she'd see them next time. She turned to the speaker to apologize: "I'm sorry, Anita, it isn't you. I'm just really upset; I just found out that my committee isn't recommending me for renewal — they said they would recommend probation instead."

"Oh! That's too bad. You didn't have any warning?" Anita asked, her voice full of concern.

"No, I was assured as recently as last Friday by my committee chair that all was well." Jessie gulped.

"Well, for what it's worth, I hear stories all the time from women students about how inhospitable this place is for them. I'm not really surprised. It's a hard time to be looking for another position, though. I just went through it before coming here. You learn to draw on your resources."

"Really? You?" Jessie asked.

"Yes, it's a sobering event. I wondered if I should do something else, but this position came along. You know, faculty on this campus are also homophobic, especially some of the men. I've heard their comments," she added. "Listen, I've got to run, but if you need to talk, just give me a call."

Jessie stood there for a few minutes before gathering up her things to go home. She felt a tiny bit better to know that someone else recognized the hostile environment of Burford, but she couldn't shake her feeling of betrayal. Why had Denise said everything was okay? Surely Denise didn't think the committee's action was supportive. If her committee couldn't support her wholeheartedly, what chance did she have with the administration? Anita's comment about homophobia echoed inside her, and she thought about who was on the college committee to review her committee's recommendation. Most likely the very homophobic male faculty of whom she had spoken. And what could have happened since last Friday? Had someone gotten to her committee?

When Lynn arrived at home, Jessie was sitting in the darkened living room and didn't even greet Lynn with her usual happy-to-see-you smile.

"You heard from your committee? They didn't recommend you for renewal even after what Denise said?" Lynn said, coming over to her.

Jessie got up and buried her face in Lynn's shoulder. She started crying and couldn't even get out the word *probation.*

At last, Jessie blurted out the whole thing and sank into a depressed silence.

Lynn held her and tried to comfort her. She went into the small kitchen and heated up some soup for dinner. Jessie barely ate. Lynn was clearly upset, but nothing she could do seemed to help. Finally, Lynn went up to bed alone.

Jessie roused herself and called Carmel Gratio, one of the untenured faculty members she thought she could trust, and cried on the phone to her for an hour. "Oh, Carmel, I'm sorry. It's very late and you were already in bed when I called."

"That's okay. You *are* going to fight this decision, aren't you?" Carmel said. "I wrote you a supportive letter, and there must be others."

Jessie could hear the weariness in her voice. "I guess I could try and get some more support. Maybe not enough of the untenured faculty wrote letters because they didn't think their letters would count. I can also contact the lawyer that helped with the grievance last year."

"Yes," Carmel said. "Let me know what I can do to help."

When Jessie finally went to bed, it was late. A plan would allow her some reason to get out of bed. She felt a little better but maybe that was because she had just spent so many hours crying. She felt as if someone had taken a hammer and with one well-aimed blow had shattered her world. They didn't even have to murder her to get rid of her.

CHAPTER 13

Later Jessie got a copy of the letter Denise Oberon had sent with the committee's recommendation to the administration. She was shocked to read that Denise had written that the probation recommendation had been thoroughly explained to Jessie and she hadn't even protested and therefore it was assumed that she accepted the committee's findings as accurate. She knew she would have to keep clear of Denise. She was so angry that she felt like smashing her in the face. It was clear that military culture and this sorority-style campus had nothing much to do with each other. Jessie felt completely out of place. She didn't seem to have a clue as to what was going on, nor did they seem to understand her. In that respect, they were right; she didn't belong here, but not because she wasn't a competent administrator, teacher and scholar — those charges she would have to fight.

Jessie arranged to meet with Lucy Taft, who was one her committee members, to see if she could find out more about the complaints against her. The actual letters were secret, so she could not know the contents or who her detractors were, but Jessie knew that Lucy had seen them. Nonetheless, she wasn't very forthcoming. As they sat in a booth in the back of the student union, Jessie asked, "What's going on, Lucy? Denise told me on Friday not to give a minute's worry as to whether the committee would recommend renewal. Then on Monday, she said you all were recommending probation."

Lucy looked uncomfortable. Her only comment was, "She said that, did she?"

"But Lucy, I was working closely with you. I thought you supported me. Didn't you review my file for the administrative area?" Jessie said, trying to keep her voice even.

"I wrote you a good recommendation, but you know, I've been so busy,. I haven't been able to keep close tabs on what Denise is doing. I can well imagine that you're upset." Lucy gave her a sympathetic smile.

Upset! You mealy-mouthed shit! Jessie seethed inside. She sat there and tried to calm herself and to believe in Lucy's good will, but her patience was about gone.

Jessie took a deep breath. "I talked to Carmel Gratio and she thought I should fight this decision. I can't believe that all of the women's studies faculty responded negatively to my review. I've been thinking about having a women's studies retreat to see if I can get support."

"I don't think you should do it, Jessie. I know these women. They'll just have a feeding frenzy. You'll really leave yourself open." Lucy seemed uncomfortable, shifting her Birkenstocks under the booth.

Just then Chris walked up with a tray and said cheerfully, "Hi, you two. Are you discussing business or can I join you?"

Before Jessie could say anything, Lucy smiled and said, "We're about through. Sit down."

Jessie understood that she had just been dismissed. The last thing she wanted was to share any of this with Chris. "Oh, look at the time," she said, masking her anger and gathering her things. "I have to get back to my office."

Jessie decided to go ahead with the retreat anyway. What options did she have? She thought that only a concentrated effort by the women's studies faculty could save her. If she could get them to say that the committee's decision hadn't represented their wishes, maybe they could get the probation idea dumped and just recommend that her contract be renewed. Jessie met with Carmel, who as far as Jessie could tell was well liked, and asked her to be the facilitator of the meeting. They had carefully planned to have a discussion of a mission statement for Women's Studies and specific ways people could be involved with the program. Jessie thought that if people took more responsibility for the program, she could make them feel more empowered, especially the junior faculty.

When the retreat evening rolled around, Jessie got there early to set up and watch the food service people put out the buffet dinner. She had gone to the trouble of contacting Dean Whiffle to request money to feed the group. She had told him that the purpose of the retreat was to work on the program review which would occur during the following year. She had gathered samples of mission statements and organizational structures from other women's studies programs and had them ready to hand out. She put on a tape of an inspiring quotation from one of her lesbian-feminist heroes, Audre Lorde, to start the meeting.

To start out, Carmel led them in a brainstorming session. What, she asked, would they like to see women's studies do in the future? She wrote down the suggestions with a marking pen on the big pad of paper set up on an easel in the "drawing room" of the elegant old house which Burford used for such occasions. All was going well; everyone seemed cooperative and Jessie started to relax. The next item on the agenda was to divide into small groups to discuss the mission statements and organizational structures with a view to reorganizing the governance of Burford's own Women's Studies Program. Jessie had supplied a draft of how she thought it might work for their consideration. If she could get them to see that they were all in this together, maybe they could save her.

As Carmel was explaining that they were going to break up into small working groups, Lucy raised her hand. "Thank you for these suggestions, Jessie. I can see your ideas about organizational structure clearly. These are very helpful, but I don't think this is what is wanted."

After a moment's silence, Carmel tried again. "If everyone would divide themselves up into small groups of four or five, I'll come around and tell you what to work on, unless you have a preference. Some people can go into the other room."

No one moved. Lucy adjusted her vest and long jean skirt, then cleared her throat. "I think I expected something different from you, Jessie. I expected you to be a strong leader — to unify us."

Jessie thought, here it goes. Lucy warned her, but she didn't expect her to start it. She said aloud, "In my interview, I said I would work on organizing seminars for the women's studies faculty to share their work with one another and that I would expand the curriculum, which I did."

Carmel, in her peacemaker role, chimed in, "I think we didn't really communicate to Jessie what we wanted her to do. We seemed to want one thing at the time and now we want another."

But even Carmel's attempt couldn't stop the meeting from deteriorating. Their carefully worked out agenda was lost. It was all Jessie could do to sit and listen to their criticisms.

"You should have known that things weren't going well," Denise said. "Why, when I was directing the program, I called up all the department chairs about the classes. I never talked to so many of the old boys in all my years here."

Fuming, Jessie listened. She had feared that Denise would use this as an opportunity to show everyone how good she really had been, even though it really didn't have much to do with Jessie. "Denise," she answered, "I thought we *were* working together closely. Why wouldn't you say something if you felt that way? After all, we spent a lot of time planning the faculty seminars together."

"Why didn't you ask me?" Denise shot back.

Jessie tried to keep calm. She didn't want to get into a shouting match. For her that would be another loss of face.

As one tenured faculty member after another said their piece, Jessie watched Chris to see if she would join in, but she said nothing, just sat there quietly. She neither defended nor attacked Jessie, keeping herself clear of the whole ordeal.

Finally, one of the food service people came in and said dinner was ready. Jessie knew they wanted to clean up and be on their way, and she had had enough of the retreat. She rose and said, "Yes, let's eat," allowing the women next to the French doors to be first into the buffet line.

Jessie stood in the line silently, listening to the others. Carmel came up next to her. "I'm sorry, Jessie. I tried to get them back on track."

Jessie nodded at her numbly. When she got through the line, she found a place at the bottom of the stairs in the hall. She couldn't bear going back into the drawing room with the others. Jessie knew that it was over. There would be no rally to defend her.

Later, on her way out the door, one of the untenured women came over and gave her a sympathetic hug. "I thought about your being new here, and all this didn't seem right," but she hadn't said anything to the group. Jessie wasn't as crushed as she had imagined she would be; she was angry at the treachery. She had pulled inside herself, covering her ire with a mask of coolness, a trick she'd learned to evoke in the years of constant moving.

When Jessie left the building and went out to the parking lot, Lucy was waiting for her. "I had an idea," she said brightly. "You could give all the courses Women's Studies teaches in other departments a Women's Studies number — cross-list them."

These people have no shame, she thought. If only it was so simple. But she said, "Thanks, Lucy, I'll see what I can do. That's just a matter of checking with the different department chairs and filling out forms," and she turned and got into her car.

The drive home took about ten minutes. Jessie kept thinking about what had happened. The evening had been an overwhelming defeat of any expectation that the group could be pulled together on her behalf. She couldn't see anything feminist about their attack on her. The only unity had been with the senior faculty firmly against her. The split between the junior and senior faculty remained. The whole evening had certainly been a vote of no confidence in her leadership. Not much hope left now for salvaging the situation.

When she drove up to the house, the porch light was on, and Jessie knew Lynn would be waiting. As she gathered her things and strode up the stairs and onto the porch, she knew that this time she wouldn't cry. She was furious. All her ideas about justice and feminism had been violated. Who did these people think they were?

She slammed the door and threw her things on the floor, tossing her coat on the couch. Lynn took one look at her and said, "That bad, huh?"

Jessie nodded. She was so angry that she didn't feel like talking. She needed to do something with her anger and she didn't want to take it out on Lynn, so she got out the vacuum and started cleaning the floors, sending the cats running. She had learned a long time ago that vacuuming shut out everything. There was just you and the enemy cat hair everywhere. Lynn left her alone until her anger was spent and she had worn herself out.

Then Lynn came over, put the vacuum away and said, "Okay, go take a shower and then we'll talk."

Jessie ran the shower hard, and in the steaming water, she let out several screams, hoping the shower would drown out her anguish. Finally dry and in her purple velour bathrobe, she went to tell Lynn what had happened.

On Monday morning Denise seemed to be waiting when Jessie reached her office. "Well, see, Jessie, it will be all right if you'll just do what we told you to do," she chirped.

Jessie had never seen Denise so upbeat. Under the circumstances, the only thing that could make her so happy was that she was enjoying Jessie's situation. She probably felt vindicated for whatever slight she perceived Jessie had committed, Jessie thought with anger.

Jessie remembered how the women had ignored her plans. Certainly they put her in her place as an untenured director. She said, "The retreat showed that I can't work with you all," and she did the same thing that Carrie had done before her. She turned the key in her lock, went in and shut the door behind her, leaving Denise sputtering. She was shaking she was so angry. Denise certainly didn't need to murder anyone for revenge if that was the motive of the killer. She seemed able to enforce her will with a nasty civility. If this continued, she'd be lucky to get out of here herself without doing violence. Jessie supposed that Denise would probably go right to the college committee and say, "Forget probation. She's not repentant or cooperative," but she wasn't sure she cared.

Not long after the incident with Denise, Lucy came by. "I'm sorry, Jessie, I tried to warn you," she said, shuffling her Birkenstocks.

"Yes, Lucy, you did, but you didn't say you'd start it," Jessie replied icily.

"Well, being director is a tough job. I wouldn't want to do it. I'll see you later when you're more reasonable," she said and turned and left.

Jessie realized too late that Lucy had held a grudge all this time over the unaffiliation issue. "I must have made her look bad to the other women and the rest of the department," Jessie said to no one. How did I get into this mess?

CHAPTER 14

Over the next few weeks, it was only her work with the lawyer and Lynn's support that kept Jessie sane. On the Friday before the renewal decisions were to be announced, Denise popped into her office.

"Just wanted to know if you wanted company tomorrow when you go to your mailbox at noon to get your letter," she said. "I could get champagne."

The idea that Denise actually entertained the idea that she might get renewed was a surprise. Then she remembered Denise saying not to worry about the committee recommending her — and her believing it.

Perverse sense of humor, she thought. For a moment, she considered picking her up and tossing her out of her office, but instead she said, "Oh, is that how renewals are done? They'll be in the mailboxes tomorrow by noon? I didn't know."

"Oh yes, tenure too. Many a victory or a defeat party started at the mailboxes," she said.

"Well, thanks anyway. I'll manage," Jessie said.

After Denise had left, Jessie shuddered, remembering a friend who had planned a party to celebrate the defense of his dissertation. They had waited in the hall, champagne in hand, for the chair of his committee to emerge with the news. When the chair came out she apologetically told everyone that he hadn't passed. She had tried to tell him that he wasn't ready to defend. Jessie could imagine that scene replayed at the mailboxes of Burford with herself as the failure. Really, did Denise think she was crazy or did she just feel like gloating?

That Saturday she and Lynn drove up to school and collected her mail. She was happy to see that no one was in the hall. She grabbed the stuff in her box and returned to the waiting car. When she ripped open the envelope, she wasn't surprised to see that the administration had turned down her renewal, saying she was inadequate as director and teacher — nothing about her scholarship. She wasn't surprised, but she had retained a tiny bit of hope. Why else would they have made a special trip to collect the darn thing? She did feel some relief, though. The waiting was over. Lynn had made an appointment for that very afternoon with Edwina Andrews, the lawyer who had handled the other faculty case against Burford. Unlike Jessie, she'd been skeptical.

Jessie showed Lynn the letter. "Okay, now we go to plan B," she said. "They really are obnoxious, aren't they? Your committee said your teaching was fine. They just lumped everything together to make certain they could get rid of you. Let's go for lunch. We have plenty of time before our appointment."

They were ushered into a small office in an old house. The furniture was practical but not ostentatious. Edwina greeted them and asked them to sit down in the two chairs in front of her desk.

"Tell me about your situation," she said.

"Well, I'm the Director of Women's Studies at Burford. I've just been denied renewal. I was given a fourth-year in place of my first review. I think you have some experience with that from a previous case."

Looking at Jessie and Lynn, she asked, "Do you think that the denial had anything to do with homophobia?"

"Very possibly," Jessie said. "I brought along all the papers connected with the case and the faculty procedures manual. I have one really ugly flyer done by the student prankster group naming me as a lesbian, but nothing written from faculty or administration indicating homophobia."

Edwina adjusted the cuff on her white blouse and said, "Well, we can check into that. You said you just received your denial? You haven't gone through the grievance process then?"

"No," Jessie answered.

"Well, that's the first thing you have to do. I

can't come into the process until you do. File a grievance on the basis of your advanced review in your first year. Once you've gone through the process, we can go from there. Leave these materials with me and I'll look them over. Call me at the beginning of next week, and I'll help you with your grievance letter if you like."

Jessie hated filing the grievance. Except for the lawyer's help with her letter, she had to figure out how to do everything herself. She even sent out a general appeal to the women's studies faculty and students asking for letters of support to go to the administration. Of course, she discovered that was a futile effort. The administration made it clear that they believed such letters to be nonobjective, after the fact and not worth their consideration. The whole nightmare continued for Jessie. She already felt shamed, although Lynn kept telling her that she hadn't done anything wrong.

Her sleeping had gotten worse, and she was losing weight. It didn't help that the siren posed across from their bedroom went off frequently. Whenever that happened Jessie was jolted awake, her pulse pounding. As a child living on the military base, the wail of the sirens had signaled a plane crash. Desperately, she would try to figure out if her father was on duty. If he was, it could be him. Now whenever the siren went off, she was overwhelmed by fear. It always took her a few minutes to realize where she was, and there would be little hope for sleep that night.

The dreams started. She was a small child and her mother was very ill. If she was good enough and quiet enough, her mother would get better. Sometimes her mother would smile at her efforts to make her better, and Jessie would think she *was* getting better. But then she would see that her mother was dying. When Jessie would wake up sweating and afraid, Lynn would rouse herself long enough to hold her and try to get her back to sleep.

When the grievance committee found in her favor, the administration thanked the committee and then denied that their findings were valid. Finally, the lawyer could come onto campus and examine the file. She had completed all the grievance steps provided by Burford.

Jessie was outside when she heard the telephone ringing. She ran in to grab it before the answering machine picked up. "Hello," she said, gasping for breath. It was Edwina Andrews. "Oh, Edwina, what did you find?"

"I didn't find the evidence of discrimination because you are lesbian as we had hoped — nothing so simple. I found one really nasty letter, though," Edwina said.

"From whom?" Jessie asked.

"A Chris Stendal."

"Chris? Oh no . . ." Jessie didn't want to believe it, and there was a long silence.

"Jessie, are you there?"

"What did it say?" Jessie plunked herself down on the floor next to the wall phone, remembering the

111

day she had asked Chris if she had written her a letter and Chris's affirmative reply.

"She said you were unfit to be director, that you were 'unreasonably suspicious.' I asked Dean Whiffle why her letter would be taken seriously since she so obviously disliked you, and he said that since she was the closest person to the program, she should know. I'm going to write a letter of protest so it will be on record, but it isn't hopeful that they will change their minds," Edwina said with a sigh. "I've seen this kind of jealousy and infighting between women before. From your response, I guess this didn't make you feel any better."

Jessie sat slumped against the wall, the phone in the crook of her neck, her hands over her face. She said, "No, I should have known. All the signs were there, but I didn't let myself see it — paranoid, huh! Hell! What with the murders, the pornographic flyer, the threats and the graffiti on my door, how dare she? And there's nothing I can do about it? And the administration bought this crap! She's just going to get away with this?"

"I'm sorry. There's nothing we can legally do about it. We can take the college to court over the irregularities in the review process. They aren't going to be so quick to settle this time since they've settled once recently. It sets a bad precedent. Yours isn't my only case Burford has threatening to sue them this year. If we can't show discrimination — thus a lot of unfavorable publicity — it won't be an easy case to win or even to try to get a settlement out of court."

"The other case is Carrie Small's, isn't it? She told me she was seeing a lawyer. What do you advise me to do?" Jessie asked.

Edwina answered, "For contract violation cases, the court is often more sympathetic if you're unemployed for a period of time, so you might want to wait and see what happens in the job market. You think about it and let me know. We have several years to decide. You still have another year at Burford to look for a job."

"I had an interesting conversation with President Whiffle. "She told me that there's a Board of Trustees mandate not to keep more than fifty percent of any new faculty. She was very matter-of-fact about it."

After Jessie hung up, she sat there stunned. It had been Chris all along. She was really good — what a wonderful way to discredit her — "unreasonably suspicious." Once the administration bought that, no one would listen to her. It was perfect.

When Lynn came home from work and Jessie told her about Chris's letter, Lynn said, "I'm not surprised — that bitch! The administration swallowed it too, and the lawyer says there's nothing we can do, hmm? You know that place that blew up in Mexico from gasoline in the sewers? How about I go over to Burford and try it there? They'd never know what hit 'em. Or here's a better idea. Let's call Act Up and have them come in drag to move you out of your office during graduation. Can't you see the administration's faces when a truck full of queens pulls up onto the quad where the ceremonies are going on — all those prissy students and their parents — and they start loading up books? The more outrageous, the better!"

Jessie laughed, and for a moment, she considered it.

CHAPTER 15

Jessie felt sentenced to serve her last year at Burford. With the short notice, she hadn't been able to find another job, and they couldn't afford for her to just quit. It would be better for her career if she kept the position while she sought another. Now she would have to do damage control and limit prospective employers' contact with Burford faculty. Carmel Gratio had agreed to serve as a reference, but Jessie couldn't trust the rest of them. She hated feeling trapped. She did the best she could, trying to focus on her teaching and working in the office as little as possible. She quit attending meetings and told the women's studies faculty that they would have a meeting if anyone saw fit to call one, if there were any issues anyone thought were important. Just as she suspected, no one had. Although her office was right next to Chris's and they lived next door to her and Pam, Jessie made a point to stay away from them. When she occasionally ran into Chris, she would say hello perfunctorily and move on.

According to Betty, the police were no closer to solving the murders, and Jessie tried to stay alert. She still suspected Chris had something to do with them, but she had no real evidence. And since she'd been labeled as "overly suspicious," who would believe her? Accusing Chris would look like sour grapes.

Lynn was running an evening series of safety planning workshops, and Jessie had attended one or two now that she was out of the loop at Burford. It was strange to have so much time on her hands, but she wanted to support Lynn.

Lynn had one evening blocked out for domestic violence training for the local police, and they had the opportunity to meet Detective Carin.

He approached them afterwards. "That was an interesting session, Ms. Perry. Some of that information could be quite helpful."

Lynn smiled and introduced Jessie.

"Aren't you the detective who was investigating Joyce Barnette's murder?" Jessie asked. "Any more progress on that case?"

"Why do you ask? Did you read about the case or

115

do you have a more personal connection to it?" The detective had no gray in his dark hair and the deepest blue eyes she had ever seen. He looked from Jessie to Lynn.

"Well, I'm always interested in such cases," Lynn said. "Most women who are murdered die by the hand of someone who has been romantically involved with them, but in this case, it's a little closer to home. Jessie and I had just moved here when she was murdered."

"Something you said actually got me thinking about the Barnette case," he said. "You said perpetrators of domestic violence are always possessive — that they don't take to anyone either supporting or opposing their victim and that either of these actions may lead to violence against these outside persons. We know Joyce Barnette was lesbian. Do the same sorts of things apply to violence in lesbian relationships?"

Lynn nodded. "Yes, and in the Barnette case, we have another suspicious death among her friends occurring not long after."

"Do you mean Georgia Swain's accident?" he said, looking up sharply.

Lynn nodded. "That's the one.:

Jessie said, "I'm the one who found her, and I don't think it was an accident, but I told all this to the police already. The two deaths seem related."

"Well, you've both given me something to think about. Thank you."

As the year wore on, the notices for Jessie's

position went out. Denise brought the schedule for the candidate visits to Jessie's office.

"Jessie, do you have a minute," she said, poking her head around the door.

"What can I do for you?" Jessie said mildly.

"I wanted to give you the schedule for the candidate visits and ask if you'd be willing to talk to them," Denise said sincerely.

"Sure, I'll talk to them," Jessie said.

"You can even take them to lunch if you like. The dean will pay for it." She handed the schedules to Jessie. "Will those dates be okay?"

Jessie glanced at the sheets. "Fine," she said. "But only two candidates? I thought you were interviewing three."

"We are. The other one is Chris Stendal. You won't have to talk to her."

After Denise left, Jessie just stood there shaking her head. So Chris had done it. She had gotten her Ph.D., discredited Jessie and was applying for her position. Why wasn't she surprised?

Jessie met with both of the candidates. At the dean's expense, she took each to the local upscale restaurant, which tried hard to maintain itself in Victorian splendor. The food was good, and Jessie enjoyed telling each candidate what she thought of Burford and Women's Studies and charging lunch to the college. Still, she tried to be as objective as she could. Her military background demanded no less. Both candidates were personable and each seemed to sympathize with Jessie's plight. Both were senior professors and could take leave to try out Burford. One had another offer, however, and after listening to Jessie's story said she would take the other position. She thought she wouldn't fit well into Burford.

Things were even worse between Jessie and Chris. Jessie no longer made any pretense of even being civil to her. Usually, if she came in contact with her, she just ignored her. As it turned out, the position was not offered to Chris, and Jessie felt a small bit of satisfaction. One afternoon Chris came storming into Jessie's office.

"Why wasn't I invited to the Women's Studies picnic?" she demanded loudly.

"I'm doing it a little differently this year," Jessie said. "It's just going to be for students and the faculty who judged our creativity contest rather than for the community at large."

"But," Chris said, "the Women's Center Director has always come to the picnic. I'm a co-sponsor."

"I checked that," Jessie said with some satisfaction. "Your name is on one of the awards, but the whole thing comes out of my budget."

Chris turned, left the room and came back with Denise in tow.

Pulling a little rank, Jessie thought.

Denise said, "I didn't get an invitation to the picnic, either."

"As I was explaining to Chris, only the students and faculty involved with judging the awards are invited. It's my going-away party, too," she added. "Surely I can invite whoever I want."

Chris made one last try, "But we're supposed to work together."

Jessie looked her straight in the eye and said, "We haven't worked together all year. Why pretend now? Do you want to discuss our differences?"

At that, both Denise and Chris left her office.

When Jessie got to her office that Monday, the police were everywhere. The small, dimly lit hall was full of people going in and out. She was stopped by a uniformed policewoman who asked her business.

"I'm Jessie Batelle, Director of Women's Studies, and my office is right over there," she said, pointing just past the crowd by Chris's office. "What's going on?"

"You can go through. They'll be wanting to question you," the policewoman replied.

Jessie peered into Chris's office as she walked by. A man in a raincoat was taking pictures. Something was hanging in front of the windows at the far end of the long narrow office. Jessie gasped and her knees buckled. She sat with a thunk on the floor, dropping her keys and briefcase. Someone came and helped her get up, go into her office and onto a chair.

"Quite a shock?" The man who helped her into her office stood beside her. The light from her big windows was streaming into the hallway, and she realized that her office had been opened.

"I'm Detective Carin," the man said, showing her his identification. "We've met. You're Jessie Batelle, Director of Women's Studies."

Jessie nodded dumbly with the image of what she had seen flashing before her. It was Chris, hanging from the ceiling tile supports with her academic hood twisted around her neck. The vibrant colors of the hood contrasted with her darkened face.

"When you feel like you can talk, I'd like to ask you some questions," he said gently.

Jessie wasn't sure how much time had passed before she could respond. She remembered taking her black leather gloves off, stuffing them into her pocket and slipping her navy wool blazer off and letting it fall around her on the chair. She was having yet another one of her hot flashes.

Finally, she was able to say to the Detective sitting across from her in one of her chairs, "Yes, I remember you. What did you want to know?"

"Did you know Chris Stendal well, Ms. Batelle?" he asked.

Jessie hesitated. "Well, yes and no," she replied, wondering how much to say. She still felt daunted by male authority, even though she'd met him before and he seemed younger than she. Lynn was better at this than she was, and she tried to think about what Lynn would say.

"Yes and no?" Detective Carin asked.

"I've been at Burford for about two years. Last year, when I was new, Lynn and I did a lot of things socially with Chris Stendal. Our jobs also complement each other — Women's Programming and Women's Studies. But I really didn't know her very well. Look —" she interrupted herself. "Do you suspect that someone did this to Chris or did she commit — "

"Suicide?" he filled in for her. "We aren't sure. We're investigating all angles. There was a note, but it wasn't signed. You said when you were new, did something change after you'd been here longer?"

"This last year we haven't spoken much to each other — only when our jobs made it imperative. I haven't made any secret of how angry I've been with her although I never confronted her." Her little alarm went off in her head when she said this, and she knew it was one of the things Lynn wouldn't say, but it was too late.

"Why, what happened?" he asked, his blue eyes watchful.

Jessie sighed, shifted in her chair and ran a hand over her purple corduroy pants. "I was up for contract renewal this year; the process was not clear. I wasn't recommended for renewal. I wasn't allowed to see the file so I didn't really know what the problem was. I hired a lawyer and she found a very damaging letter. It was from Chris Stendal."

"You had no indication before that she opposed you?"

"Not really. She seemed more distant, but once when I asked, she said she was just tired — she was finishing her Ph.D. She graduated in December." Jessie's voice broke, remembering the hood twisted around Chris's neck. She covered her face with her hands as if to block out the sight.

The detective said gently, "I know this is hard right now, but just a couple more questions. What did you do when you found out that Chris had opposed you?"

"I really didn't do anything. There was nothing I could do. My lawyer asked the dean why Chris Stendal's letter counted so much since it seemed unfounded and a personal attack. He said Chris should know since she was the closest to the Women's Studies Program. I wasn't supposed to know what anyone had written. I filed a grievance on procedural grounds, but that didn't change anything." Jessie's voice trailed off, not wanting to relive the painful incident.

"You say you never confronted her?" he asked, turning his blue eyes on her.

"I don't like unpleasantness. I couldn't see what would be accomplished." Another legacy of being a military brat, she thought. "I was so hurt. I felt betrayed. I had trusted Chris, and she had never indicated that she had any problems with the way I was running the program."

"So why do you think she wrote the damaging letter?"

"I think she wanted my job. She wasn't eligible for it when I came — she didn't have her Ph.D. then — but after February she was." She frowned.

"So she got her Ph.D. in February. Did she have a good chance of getting your job?" he asked.

"Well, she applied, but she didn't get it. You don't think that she was so distraught that — Did the note give any indication?"

Detective Carin answered, "I'm afraid I can't release that information right now. Just a couple more questions. Where were you last night?"

"I was home," she answered.

"Was there anyone with you?"

"Lynn, Lynn Perry." As she said this, she looked over at him and watched his very blue eyes to see his reaction. He didn't show any uncomfortableness.

He said, "We'll contact her later. Did Ms. Stendal have enemies that you know of?"

"I'm afraid I've already told you that I could be

considered an enemy, but killing her? No, I wouldn't kill her." Although Lynn had some pretty good fantasies about it, she thought, something she did know not to say. "Yes, Chris has some enemies, but it's hard to imagine anyone actually killing her. With the number of suspicious deaths we've had this past year, I guess that's a real possibility. Actually, before this happened, I thought it was Chris who — " She stopped, unable to continue. She closed her eyes and swallowed hard. After a moment she said, "You're working on the other cases."

"Yes, and this may be connected. We'll stop now and I'll talk to you again later." He glanced at his watch.

"I think I'll go home — I'm not teaching today. Is my secretary in?"

Snapping his notebook closed, he said, "She was pretty shaken. She's the one who found the body. She went home."

"Do you want me to leave my office open?" Jessie said, putting her jacket back on and retrieving her keys and briefcase.

"We're finished in here," he said. "You can lock up."

Jessie didn't remember much about the ten-minute walk down the hill to the little faculty house. When she got there, she took off her jacket and gloves and tossed them on a chair with her briefcase. She noticed the house was cold and turned up the heat. She wanted to call Lynn but knew she was in court doing legal advocacy with her battered women until late in the afternoon. She needed to think about this latest development.

She could use a drink. She checked under the sink where they kept the bottles but saw nothing but cleaning supplies. She tried the refrigerator for wine, coming up empty. Sighing, she filled the teakettle with water and put it on to heat. In the cabinet over the stove she rummaged around, finding some of her favorite Earl Grey tea in the back. She found her "Adam was a rough draft" cup and then sat at the table in the small dining room, waiting for the water to boil.

A bed of jonquils grew just outside the window where the hillside and house met so that the flowers actually appeared to be growing window-high, even though there was a space between the two. The flowers had been a welcome surprise in the small neglected yard. The pleasure they usually gave her was dimmed by the ugly events of the morning. The whistle from the kettle broke into her thoughts, and she went into the kitchen to make her tea.

She poured the hot water over the tea bag. The steam rose with the comforting perfumy essence. She took her cup into the small living room and sat down in the blue recliner. The big gray cat snuggled into her lap. The calico perched on the back of the recliner after an enthusiastic greeting of small squeaky sounds, and the kitten launched herself into Jessie's lap, pushing the big gray over to make room.

Incorrigible, Jessie thought. They don't take no for an answer.

Jessie enjoyed watching the kitten challenge the big cats, assault their dignity, and then purr and rub.

It was hard for her to be mad at the kitten for long, though she had just about destroyed their house plants, thinking they were her own private playground. About a year old, she climbed the ficus, the Christmas cactuses and hibiscus, breaking off leaves and branches as no other kitten before her had done. When she was scolded, she would purr and rub as she did with the big cats. Charmed as Jessie was by her, the state of her plants made her sorry they had taken her in.

She realized that thinking about the kitten was a nice distraction from the horrible scene she had witnessed that morning. She tried to put the image of Chris hanging from the ceiling out of her mind. She needed to figure out what was going on. If Chris hadn't been responsible for the other deaths, who had?

Jessie picked up her notebook and pen from the coffee table to add to the notes she'd been keeping. She remembered the day she was introduced to the faculty by Chris when the promise of their friendship was still tangible. It all seemed hard to believe.

CHAPTER 16

At the sound of the porch door being pulled shut, she blinked, startled. When Lynn walked in and switched on the light, Jessie realized she'd been sitting there for hours and must have fallen asleep. She sat up and the notebook slipped off her lap and fell to the floor. The calico leapt from the stool at her feet. Lynn put down her briefcase. She was clearly surprised to see Jessie sitting in the dark.

"What's wrong?" she blurted out.

"Well, I got to work this morning and police were everywhere. Chris is dead," Jessie said, getting up and burying her head into Lynn's shoulder, the tears beginning to come as Lynn opened her arms to her. Jessie wasn't sure why she was crying. She had, after all, thought Chris had been responsible for Joyce's and Georgia's deaths. Was this guilt at thinking such a thing and then seeing Chris hanging there?

Jessie just stood there and cried on Lynn's shoulder. When she could talk again, Lynn directed her to the couch and sat down next to her, handing her a tissue from the box on the coffee table. "Can you tell me about it? How did it happen?" Lynn said, concern in her voice.

"She was hanging there — her hood — her academic hood around her neck." Jessie sobbed. "I don't think it was suicide."

"Hanging there? In her office? From the ceiling?" Lynn's jaw dropped.

"Yes, it was awful. Her face was all black."

"How did Chris's office look? Did it look like there had been a struggle?" Lynn asked.

Jessie shook her head, "I didn't see much after I saw her hanging there. Mostly, the same piles of books and papers on the floor and desk were around. Now that I think of it, the office seemed neater than usual."

"Was there something Chris could have stood on to reach the ceiling? She's not very tall," Lynn commented.

"I don't remember seeing anything. I've stood on the built-in under the window to water my hanging plants before, but I don't think Chris could reach the ceiling supports from hers. She's so much shorter than I am."

"You said the police were there? What do they think happened?" Lynn asked.

"The police detective — Detective Carin, the one we met at your workshop — said there had been a note, but it wasn't signed. They don't know yet. He questioned me. I had to tell him that there was trouble between me and Chris," Jessie said, pushing the calico away. She was purring and trying to shove her way onto Jessie's lap.

Lynn smiled knowingly. "Yes, of course you would. Did he seem to take what you said seriously — you're not a suspect?"

Jessie gave up and let the calico settle on her lap. "He asked where I was last night. I told him I was with you and he said he'd be contacting you. He just said he'd talk to me more later. I was pretty upset and he seemed understanding — even about our relationship. It seemed fairly routine, not very different than the questions about Georgia's death."

"Well, good. It sounds as if you did the right thing. They'd probably find out about Chris's involvement in your non-renewal anyway." Lynn paused, then laughed with recognition, "Unless, of course, Burford continues to try to keep that quiet, to protect their lousy review process. It'll be good for them to have the police poking around in their muck. Maybe we should contact Edwina to tell her to renew her efforts to get you a settlement. I'd still like to blow the place up."

"You're outrageous!" Jessie said, managing a little smile. She became suddenly quiet and glanced away.

"What are you thinking?" Lynn asked.

"About Pam, wondering how she's taking this. And I had the oddest thing flash through my mind — Pam riding back to town on the bike trail with a golf club the day that Georgia died."

"You never mentioned that before. You passed her on your way to meet Georgia?" Lynn said, frowning.

"Yes, I remembered she seemed a little startled to see me."

"There's something we're not putting together here. What do you know about Pam and Chris's relationship?" Lynn asked.

Jessie petted the calico, who was purring loudly on her lap. "I know it's been a pretty stormy one — on and off again. They had a commitment ceremony not too long after Chris came to Burford, even though they were separated when Chris arrived. That's how Chris got involved with Joyce, or at least that's what she told me when she was warning me against Joyce. She said she and Pam were living apart and not getting along, that she was lonely." She paused. "Chris did say once that she and Pam were splitting up, but they were going to continue to share the same house for a while because of all the things they had going on at the time. Chris said she couldn't afford to move out. I gather Pam didn't want to. Oh, and I saw a big bruise — Chris had a big bruise on her forehead. Chris made me promise not to mention their splitting up to anyone."

"When was this?" Lynn asked.

"Early in the spring before I found out that I wasn't renewed and that they were going to do a search for my position." Jessie shrugged.

"What happened after that? I never saw anyone move out," Lynn asked.

"Well, the next time I saw Chris, she said they'd worked everything out. They were staying together."

Just then the kitten jumped onto Jessie's lap, driving away the older cat who apparently felt herself above competition for laps or food. She left with a swat to the kitten's head and a hiss signaling her displeasure. Jessie grabbed her leg and shoved the kitten away, "Darn cat scratched me!"

Lynn ignored the fracas and said thoughtfully, "You know Pam has been in the background in all of this. "If she was violent, a batterer, let's say, she might have thought Chris was having affairs even if she wasn't, although we know that Chris *did* have a relationship with Joyce. Everyone knew about it, especially Denise who watched it from across the street. So if Pam was the batterer type, she might have gotten to the point where she felt that if she couldn't have Chris, no one could."

Jessie was incredulous. "I know battering occurs in the lesbian community, but murder?" Then she laughed. "Here I am reverting back to my idealistic view of women. Yesterday, I believed that Chris had killed Georgia and Joyce, so why not Pam?"

Lynn looked at her and said, "I see women who batter take on the same characteristics as male batterers all the time. If you talk to them on the telephone, for instance, and didn't know by their voices they were women, you wouldn't know the difference — they say the same things as the men and display the same attitudes. Pam's pretty strong, too. She'd have a good physical advantage over Chris."

Jessie cut in, "It's hard to think of Chris being battered or allowing it, though. She was independent and feisty. She gave me enough trouble."

"That would be all the worse — she'd never want anyone to know, especially being a lesbian-feminist. We've had cases where women who are lawyers or executives have been battered, and they absolutely don't want anyone to know — it doesn't fit with their image of themselves. And there's another angle here, too. Pam comes from a wealthy family. Big difference in class. Remember Pam saying that she tried to get Chris to dress better, but Chris didn't know how. Pam Effelton has a lot more money and she probably held that over Chris."

Jessie said, "Yes, these things would have made it hard for Chris to get out of the relationship."

"Let's see what we can find out about their relationship. Don't you know someone who went to school with them? Didn't they say they met in Michigan? Be careful, though. If Pam *is* behind all this, she'll act again to protect herself. I'll check through the battered women's channels to see if I can find out anything, although I doubt Chris would have gone to a shelter or used any of their services. They're not always responsive to battering in the lesbian community."

Jessie looked down at the kitten who had returned and now was sleeping soundly, sprawled the length of her lap. "What about the Burford community? Wouldn't someone know?"

"Someone might, but it might get back to Pam that you're asking questions. I can see why most

Burford faculty have their social life outside the Burford community — what an incestuous crew! We'd better let the police in on our suspicions, but they're just that — suspicions. We have no evidence to back any of this up."

Later that night after dinner, Jessie took Lynn by the hand and led her up to the bedroom and closed the door on the cats. They had one long embrace until they lost their balance and fell on the bed. Laughing, Jessie began to pull off Lynn's pants and then took off her own. Jessie unbuttoned Lynn's blouse and unfastened her bra, kissing her breasts in the process. Since Jessie didn't wear a bra, her sweater was quickly discarded, revealing her small breasts.

Skin against skin, they pulled together.in a rush, stroking and kissing each other until they were both satisfied and lay quietly side by side. Lynn reached over and turned out the light. As Jessie lay there drifting off to sleep, the image of Chris hanging in her office came back to her, and she reached for Lynn. Lynn drew her close and whispered, "It'll be all right."

CHAPTER 17

Jessie and Lynn decided to go to Chris'S funeral on Thursday morning, especially to see how Pam would react. Since Chris had died on campus, the memorial service was to be held in the college chapel, and she would be buried in the college's quaint, old cemetery. Jessie remembered seeing the small graveyard when Chris had taken her on a tour. They had laughed about old professors dying while on duty. She certainly hadn't thought it would apply to one of them. Not only had Chris died on campus, but she had died in the hood of her academic regalia.

The graves in the old cemetery dated back to the 1800s, not long after the college had moved to the hill. No one had been buried there for years. Joyce's body had gone on to her relatives in New Jersey, but a service had been held in the college chapel. Since Jessie had only been on campus a few days when Joyce died, she hadn't attended, and she had been laid up when Georgia's service took place in the college chapel.

The chapel was an imposing structure with white Greek pillars set atop several tiers of steps. Burford was no longer affiliated with any religious denomination, and the chapel was mostly used as an auditorium — a task for which it was acoustically impaired. Besides the 30-foot-high, sound-distorting ceilings, it also had rows of massive pillars which blocked the view from many of the wooden pews. Lynn and Jessie joined the solemn crowd entering the chapel, picking a pew midway back on the left-hand side and away from the pillars.

A large number of students had turned out. Chris had been well liked for her work with the women students' activist group. Pam came down the aisle flanked by Denise in gray slacks and blazer and Lucy, who still wore her long skirt and Birkenstocks. They walked slowly to the front. Pam wore an elegant black wool trousersuit, but she looked upset. Her face was swollen and puffy. Pam, Lucy and Denise sat together. Pam sobbed every once in a while during the service. Lucy handed her tissues. Jessie also saw the young woman student who had been involved with Joyce sitting in a nearby pew. Carrie Small, having been denied tenure, was now in the same position as Jessie of finishing out her contract. She sat just in front of Lynn and Jessie. Jessie had steered clear of her after Carrie had insisted on defending Chris when Jessie's contract hadn't been renewed.

As she looked around, Jessie realized that of the lesbian faculty who had been at Burford when she arrived, their number was down by half. Could it really be that they were killing each other off, or was it someone from outside? The prankster group had been keeping a pretty low profile, although she heard they'd been questioned. They had taken credit for no activities lately. But then, anyone could have picked up their flyer and put it on her car window with the threat.

Jessie tuned back into the service just as the college chaplain was extolling Chris's many contributions to the college community. In the three years Chris had been there, she had been very active. Some of the students could be heard crying. Out of the corner of her eye, Jessie saw Detective Carin standing to one side of a pillar in the back. She wondered why he was there. Probably checking on suspects, she guessed. She thought about who those would be. She and Lynn would be suspects. The student who was tricked into filing charges against Joyce by Chris might be another. The prankster group or someone like them who wanted to get rid of lesbians on campus could be considered suspects. Really, Pam Effelton would be the biggest suspect, Jessie thought. It was usually someone closely related to the victim.

The service over, people began filing out.

As they came out into the sunlight from the chapel, Jessie said, "I don't want to go to the burial, do you, Lynn?

"No, I need to check in at work. If you're going to your office now, be careful," Lynn said as she headed for her car. "I'll see you at home about six."

"See you then," Jessie said, turning to follow the brick walk to the quad.

Once in her hallway, Jessie noticed that the yellow police tape had been removed from the doorway of Chris's office. She unlocked her door and saw the enormous pile of mail in her basket and sat down to get to work. The building was quiet. Classes had been cancelled for the day. This area had an unpleasant feeling now that the occupants of the offices on both sides of Jessie had died. Even though Georgia's office housed the math department's computers, no one seemed to be there working. Hours passed while Jessie was engrossed in cleaning up the piles on her desk. She cleared the last piece of paper away and then decided to call her friend at the state university to see what was known about Chris and Pam's relationship.

"Kathy? I'm glad to find you in. This is Jessie Batelle at Burford. We've had some trouble here, and I'm trying to find out some information about Chris Stendal. You knew her when she was in graduate school there, didn't you?" Jessie asked.

"Of course. Chris was one of our graduate students. I heard that she committed suicide," her friend answered.

"That's the story they're giving out, but I don't think so. I'm wondering about her relationship with Pam. Was there ever any violence that you knew of?"

"They had a pretty stormy relationship. Once, when they were separated, Pam had been seen following Chris everywhere, pleading with her to take her back. She even hung around outside Chris's apartment since Chris wouldn't talk to her. Pam just wouldn't quit. Some of Pam's friends thought that to be spurned publicly was pretty humiliating, and they urged her to give it up."

"So what happened? Was she ever physically violent?" Jessie asked.

Just then, Jessie heard a noise and the door from what sounded like Chris's office slammed. A second later a red-faced Pam was storming into her office and standing over her. Pam grabbed the phone from Jessie and slammed it down.

"What do you think you're doing?" Pam shouted, shaking her fist in Jessie's face.

Jessie shrank from her but couldn't move out of range. She could feel the blood draining from her face.

"You bitch, I just saw her buried, and you have the nerve to question our relationship? I loved her and it's your fault she's dead — yours and all the other lesbian bitches on campus. You don't deserve to say her name! If you hadn't come here and stirred things up!" Pam leaned over Jessie, her face just a few inches away as Jessie tried to pull back.

From the doorway, Jessie heard someone saying, "Pam, I didn't know you were here. Did you come to get Chris's things?"

Pam turned and saw Sarah standing in the doorway. Pam nodded and abruptly pushed past her out the door.

Sarah looked at Jessie who had gotten to her feet.

"She's gone. She went down the hall," Sarah said. "She was pretty upset. What happened?"

"She must have overheard my phone call. I had no idea she was right next door. I'm glad you came in when you did. I was pretty scared. I wasn't sure what she was going to do."

"She was really angry." Sarah paused as if considering what to say. "Of course, she's going through a very difficult time," she said diplomatically. "I'm going to lock up now if you want company walking home."

"Thanks, that's a good idea." Jessie began gathering up her things.

Sarah and Jessie didn't say much as they walked down the hill. Jessie was still overwhelmed by her encounter with Pam. Finally, she looked over at Sarah, "How are you bearing up through all this, Sarah? It can't be pleasant for you. I hope you know that the problems between Chris and me had nothing to do with you, but it's certainly not what one would expect from women's studies faculty. Did Chris ever indicate to you that she was so depressed that she would take her life?"

Sarah shook her head, carefully stepping over a puddle of water. "Chris didn't share much of her life with me. I don't think she really trusted me. She barely let me do the routine things that a secretary ordinarily does for a program. I do know that there was some problem between her and Pam, but whether that was enough for her to take her life, I don't know."

"What kind of problem?" Jessie asked, moving over to avoid a fallen branch on the walk.

"Well you probably noticed that Pam was around campus a lot. She would call the office and want to know where Chris was, and she frequently showed up unexpectedly. It was as if she didn't trust her. It started not too long after Chris came to Burford. She had that relationship with Joyce, you know," Sarah said, reaching for the railing to steady herself on a steep part of the hill.

"Yes, I heard about that. So that was well known among Burford staff, too?" Jessie asked.

"This is such a small community, it's hard not to know, but in this case, Pam made a spectacular scene right in the Women's Center. A number of us were there for a women's studies meeting. That was back when Joyce was still an integral part of women's studies, Denise was acting director and many of the staff women came to meetings."

"No one told me about this," Jessie said as they stepped off the curb and crossed the street. "What happened?"

"Joyce and Chris were sitting on the couch together when Pam came in. Pam took one look and sort of exploded — like I suspect she did with you today. Started shouting at them. It was all Chris could do to get her to leave by going with her. Everyone was afraid that it was going to turn ugly. After that Joyce steered clear of Chris. Joyce was a special friend of mine and she told me it wasn't worth crossing Pam to continue having a relationship with Chris. Joyce hadn't known that Chris had a partner when Chris moved here. When Pam showed up, Chris continued to insist that it was all over. I think the scene with Pam and Joyce humiliated

Chris. This was her first position. She always tried so hard to make it seem as if she had everything together, and Pam blew that illusion."

"And then Chris tried to make Joyce the bad guy," Jessie said. "But how did she get everyone to accept that?"

"Well, Joyce wasn't known for her good judgment. She did have a number of unwise relationships. She had gotten on the wrong side of Denise who took Chris's part. It was all over for Joyce when the women's studies faculty got together and confronted her about her relationship with the student." They'd reached the ivy-draped Burford sign at the bottom of the hill. "Well, this is where we part," Sarah said. "See you tomorrow."

"Thanks for rescuing me," Jessie said and turned to walk the half a block to her house.

She wondered if Georgia was going to warn her about Pam, the day she was killed. Jessie glanced past her house to see if Pam was around anywhere. She could often be seen walking her dog, but Jessie didn't see her now. As she reached to open the door to her porch, Pam's large Doberman pinscher ran around the corner of the house, barking and lunging at Jessie. Jessie turned and flattened herself up against the door.

"Get back! Go away!" she cried.

As the big dog lurched up the stairs toward her, she remembered a trick she had learned when Lynn's hound dog used to jump on her too exuberantly. She raised her knee just as the dog was about to make contact and the dog fell back, off balance. Jessie quickly dropped her briefcase on the dog and let herself inside the porch, pulling the screen door firmly shut. The big dog got up, shook herself off, looked around as if she heard someone calling, then ambled off. Jessie looked out the screen and saw Pam standing in the adjacent yard with a whistle. Before she could say anything, the dog reached Pam's side and they both went into the house. Shaking with anger and fear, Jessie let herself back out the screen door and picked up her briefcase and her scattered books. She considered going over to confront Pam, but she thought better of it, remembering Pam's angry face just a half-hour ago in her office. She hoped that Lynn would be home soon.

When Lynn arrived home, Jessie was still distraught. She said angrily, "Now what?"

"Pam must have overheard me from Chris's office talking on my phone about their relationship. She actually came into my office and threatened me. Sarah saved me. I think she was going to hit me," Jessie blurted out.

"She's really out of control! I called Detective Carin. I told him about our conversation and that he might talk to Pam."

"That's not all. When I got home, her dog was waiting for me — wouldn't let me in the house. I had to knee it like I used to do with your hound. It finally left, but Pam was standing in her yard watching!"

"Maybe I should get out my old gun and shoot that dog! Where's the key to my trunk?" Lynn stormed.

"Wait! You can't do that!" Jessie cried. "Come

here and sit down with me. Calm down." Jessie reached up and pulled Lynn down beside her on the couch.

They sat for a minute, then Lynn said, "You're right. I'd probably end up shooting Pam. I'm so angry at what she's done. I want for us to be safe, and we just aren't. A better plan would be to file assault charges."

"Assault charges? Against the dog or Pam? What about contacting Burford security about her coming into my office?"

"So far that hasn't done much. She's not really an employee, though. Now that the funeral's over, she won't really have much reason to be on campus. You said your secretary saw what happened?"

"Yes, she didn't act surprised. She said she'd seen Pam like that before," Jessie said, petting the kitten spread out on her lap.

"What did you find out on the phone?" Lynn asked.

"Well, before I was interrupted I found out that they separated while Chris was in graduate school and that Pam wouldn't let go — followed her everywhere. Kathy didn't say stalking, but it sounded close to that."

"Sounds as if we have a classic case of domestic violence here. I have Detective Carin's card here. I'll give him another call. The way things are going, it's only a matter of time before Pam becomes completely unglued. We need to make sure that we control this situation, so we don't get hurt."

CHAPTER 18

The next day when Jessie went into work Detective Carin was waiting for her. As she walked past the glassed-in area of the Women's Center and Sarah's office, she noticed him talking to Denise. Darn, she thought. Why was she here? She'd had it with Denise after the last scene when she tried to push her weight around over not being invited to the women's studies picnic and her going-away party.

Jessie tried to walk past the Center without being seen, but˙Detective Carin came out and said, "Could we talk to you in your office?"

He and Denise had followed her down the hall and waited for her to open her office. Lynn had tried to prepare Jessie for the inevitable questioning by Detective Carin since Jessie would still be a suspect, but they hadn't counted on Denise being there, too.

Detective Carin pulled up one of Jessie's chairs and motioned for Denise to take another.

"I've been getting a statement from Ms. Oberon, and I'd like to check out a few things with you, if you don't mind," he said, flipping the page on his notepad and scribbling something.

Jessie took off her coat and threw her gloves on her desk before she sat down in her chair. She turned to face them, trying to calm herself and remember the coaching Lynn had given her. She knew that Lynn had been talking with him, but her fear of authority was beginning to rise. So far there was no proof that Pam has actually committed any of the murders, and two of the deaths weren't even considered murders. Her heart already seemed to be thumping loudly and she felt a hot flash beginning to rise.

"Ms. Batelle, could you tell me again about your activities on Sunday night, the night Ms. Stendal was killed?"

Jessie cleared her throat and began, "I was home all evening with my partner, Lynn, preparing for class and watching television."

"You didn't go up to campus?" he said, raising an eyebrow.

"No." Jessie started to add something but remembered Lynn's caution to give out only the facts. She stopped herself.

"Ms. Oberon, tell her what you told me you saw

on campus that evening." Detective Carin turned to Denise.

"Well, I was coming home from the lab about ten. I walked behind this building on the side where the women's studies offices are and I saw the lights on in both Jessie's and Chris's offices," Denise said smugly, looking pointedly at Jessie.

Jessie tried not to show her alarm. Was she being accused of murdering Chris? She said, "The lights were on in my office and in Chris's?"

"How would you account for that, Ms. Batelle? Are you in the habit of leaving your lights on when you are not present?" Detective Carin's tone displayed no emotion.

"I can't. I wasn't here. I wouldn't have left my lights on. Could the janitor have been cleaning?" Jessie asked, sitting stiffly in her chair and ineffectually fanning herself with a glove. Little beads of sweat were welling up on her forehead. She glanced over at Denise who seemed to be enjoying this immensely.

"We checked on the janitor. He cleaned this building on Friday night and wasn't due to clean again until Monday night," he responded. "Do you keep your office door locked?"

"Yes, always. I was warned to because of the trouble with the prankster group, breaking in and creating problems for women's studies," Jessie said.

"Who has a key besides the janitor?"

"At least two people, and there may be others. The same key opens my office and Chris's office. The secretary, Sarah Brown, and Chris Stendal, of course, both had keys. And," she paused, looking at Denise, "since you were Acting Director of Women's Studies and used the Women's Studies office, you must have had a key."

Denise let out a little snort, as if the idea that she might have been involved with Chris's death was preposterous, and said, "I gave that key back before you arrived."

Still, she looked rattled, and Jessie was pleased to see her off guard even if only slightly. Detective Carin turned to look at Denise and asked, "What was *your* relationship with Chris Stendal like? Were you on good terms?"

Squirming slightly in her seat, Denise said, "Yes, of course, we were. When I was Acting Director, she was new, and we got along fine together. In fact, I taught her most of what she knew about women's programming."

That wasn't what Chris said, Jessie thought. She complained about having to carry both women's studies and women's programming before Jessie came. She remembered that Chris had been leery of Denise and how she used her power, but she didn't know how to bring this up to Detective Carin.

Before she could say anything, he said to Denise, "I heard that you and Chris were involved in a serious dispute that involved trying to get a women's studies faculty member fired."

"Well, I tended to agree with Chris's judgment of the situation, but that just illustrates how well we got along," Denise replied.

"And," the detective added, "that faculty member ended up murdered."

Denise's face reddened sightly and she stammered, "Surely you don't think I had anything to do with that? I'm going back to my office now. I don't have anything more to say. I just thought you'd like to know about the lights," and she smiled her disarming lopsided grin as she left.

After Denise had shut the door behind her, the detective turned to Jessie and asked, " When you came into work after Chris Stendal's death, did you notice anything missing or moved in your office?"

Jessie thought for a moment and said, "There was one odd thing. I have a small stepladder I use for watering my hanging plants and to reach the books on the top shelves. It wasn't in the corner by my desk where I usually keep it. It was behind the door. At the time, I thought maybe Sarah Brown had borrowed it, but with all the excitement I never remembered to ask her."

"Is this it?" he asked, pointing to the small three-step ladder propped up in the corner by her desk. "This may be how the murderer got the rope up in the ceiling supports."

"Murderer? You've decided it's murder, then?" Jessie asked.

"Yes, Chris wasn't tall enough to get herself up there from any of the furniture in the office. Someone else had to be involved. The murderer made a mistake. He or she should have left something that Chris Stendal could have stepped off of to hang herself. The place was entirely too tidy," he added. "Who else knew about the ladder?"

"It wasn't really visible from the doorway unless I was using it. Sarah Brown had teased me about the ladder. She was afraid I'd fall and break my neck. I guess anyone could have walked by and seen me using it. I usually leave the door open when I'm here."

"I think those are all the questions I have for today. I'm going to take your ladder with me to have it analyzed for prints," Detective Carin said. He took out some plastic gloves, slipped them on and picked up the small ladder.

As much as Jessie wanted to end the interview, she knew she needed to tell him about the deposition Jessie's lawyer would take from Pam early next week. She was reopening her attempt to get a settlement from Burford. She sighed and began to explain.

When Jessie got home that night, it was already dark. The little house had no lights on and Lynn's car wasn't parked in front. As she opened the screen door to the porch, she noticed that the front door stood ajar. Had the cats gotten out? Once, where they had lived before, the big solid wooden door hadn't been pulled all the way shut, and she and Lynn had arrived home to see the cats dashing in and out as if to say, "Look at us; see what we can do!" It had frightened both of them. They had seen too many cats killed on the busy street.

Now the door loomed open, but no cats were visible. They had either gotten out or they were hiding. If they were hiding, it meant something had scared them.

Was someone in the house?

As quietly as she could, Jessie gingerly stepped inside the door, feeling for the light switch. She flipped it, but nothing happened. Had the cats unplugged the lamp, playing a chase game and catching the cord, or had someone purposely unplugged it? She tried the porch light. It came on and shone eerily through the windows into the living room. She could make out some movement near the kitchen. She froze and whispered, "Kitty, kitty?"

Just then a large, dark figure came out of the kitchen and lunged toward her, catching her on the shoulders, pushing her backwards to the floor and knocking the wind out of her. She let out a little cry as she fell, hitting a table sharply with her head. Before she blacked out, she felt a blast of hot breath on her face.

When she came to, Lynn was standing over her and the room was bright, so bright that her eyes hurt. "Oh, Lynn," she said, "I was so frightened. Someone was in here — knocked me down. The cats — are they all right?"

"I found the calico on the refrigerator, growling. She didn't like Pam's big Doberman being in here at all. A dog that size could easily kill a cat," Lynn said, shaking her head.

"It was Pam's Doberman? How did it get in here?" Dizzy, Jessie was trying to sit up. She felt the back of her head and her fingers came away wet with blood.

Lynn motioned for her to stay where she was and went into the downstairs bathroom and returned with a wet washrag. "Here, put this on your head. You must have hit the table."

"Is the dog gone?" Jessie asked, looking cautiously around the room.

"When I came in, she pushed past me out the

door," Lynn replied. "I was pretty surprised, but she didn't threaten me. Of course, I've always liked dogs better than you have. The worst was when I found you on the floor and the calico on the refrigerator. I thought you were dead!" Lynn said as she helped Jessie to her feet and then to the couch. "Stay here and I'll look upstairs for the other cats."

Jessie sat on the couch trying to stem the blood with the washcloth, wondering if Pam had deliberately put the Doberman into the house to scare her and to harass the cats. There didn't seem to be any other explanation. She looked around and saw that her small notebook was gone from the coffee table. All her notes about the murders had been in it. Pam must have been in the house.

Lynn came back down the stairs, carrying the kitten and followed by the big gray cat. "They were cowering under the bed," she said. "For once, the kitten wasn't harassing Gremlin. I guess Pam got the word that Edwina's going to be taking a deposition from her next week, hmm? Looks like she's pretty upset about it and wants us to back off. I don't think we should say anything to her about this, just go through with the deposition." Lynn sat down on the couch next to Jessie. The kitten purred and then squirmed out of her arms as she continued, "I'm sorry she frightened you. You've had a nasty whack on the head, but I'm not sure what the police would do about this. Ask her to keep her dog under control? Of course, there is the matter of breaking and entering. I suppose she'd say we left the doors open and our cats enticed the dog in," she said in an ironic tone.

"Lynn, my notebook is gone, the one I was

keeping about the murders. Pam had to have been here. If she reads it, she'll know we suspect her. You still don't think we should call the police?"

"Let's call Detective Carin." She picked up the phone.

Jessie leaned over and put her head on Lynn's shoulder, and Lynn held her as the phone rang.

"Detective Carin, this is Lynn Perry. We've had a break-in here ... Jessie was knocked out, but she seems to be all right. We think it was Pam Effelton. I found her dog, the big Doberman, in here and Jessie's notes about the murders are missing ... okay." She hung up and said, "He'll be right over."

They just sat cuddling on the couch waiting, and it was over an hour before Detective Carin left and they could get some dinner.

"Edwina talked to me today about the deposition proceedings next week," Jessie said as they sat down to eat. "She said that depositions are a little different than court proceedings in that questions can be objected to by the college attorney, but objections just go on record. The questions must be answered anyway, and the judge decides later what's admissible."

Just then, Gremlin, recovered from the earlier incident of the dog in the house, jumped onto the table and made for Lynn's plate. Lynn reached for the squirter. "Get down, Gremlin," she said, pointing the squirter.

Gremlin took one look and plummeted off the table, coming to rest under a chair and nonchalantly giving herself a bath as if she had been there all along. She looked up with her yellow eyes as if to say, "Who me?"

Jessie laughed, "She'll be back as soon as we aren't paying attention. Anyway, on the advice of Detective Carin, I didn't tell her the real reason we wanted to start with Pam. Do you think we can carry this off? He said if it goes like we hope the police will pay for the deposition. Otherwise, this is going to be very expensive and may not get us any closer to who the murderer is or to my getting a settlement from the college."

"I think we have a good chance. Just remember not to get drawn into it. Let your lawyer and Pam do the talking. Did you and Edwina discuss strategies?" Lynn asked, keeping an eye on Gremlin.

"Yes, she said that if we could show that Chris had malice against me and that Burford knew that and still gave her letter more credibility than others, we would have grounds to push for a settlement. We already know she wanted my position. The question is, can we show that the school knew she did. One thing, though, why am I going to be present if I'm not supposed to say anything?" Jessie asked, finishing her dinner and putting down her plate for Gremlin to inspect so Lynn could eat in peace. Gremlin daintily walked over and began licking a little butter left on the plate.

"If you know that something is being left out or think of something to pursue during the testimony, you can pass your lawyer a note about questions to ask. Also unlike court proceedings, deposition questions are often open-ended. They're really fishing expeditions," Lynn answered.

Jessie sighed, "I wish you were doing this instead of me. You're more used to these situations. I'm pretty conflicted about Pam, and tonight's incident didn't help. On the one hand, I'm afraid of her, and on the other, I'd like to confront her. Who knows how I'll do in the deposition? I might be terrified and unable to help Edwina, or so angry that I'll be unable to contain myself. I've about had it with all this."

Gremlin, finished with her plate, made another assault on Lynn's side of the table. This time, Jessie grabbed her and held her for a moment, teasing her before she put her down.

"Such an old rude fat cat," she said rubbing Gremlin's head. "Why do we put up with you? We're not eating fast enough? Owners controlled by their animals. I'm sure if Pam dog is anything like you, she could claim that the dog made her do it — a new defense."

Lynn finished with her dinner and took the plate to the kitchen. "Come on, Gremlin," she said. "You're welcome to what's here — not much." Turning to Jessie, she said, "Well, maybe we can go over some possible questions that you could have ready. It'll help keep you focused. You *can* do this; It's almost over. Where's that military-brat persistence?"

CHAPTER 19

Jessie, Edwina, Pam, and the college lawyer, Al Baldwin, settled in around the oval table in the president's conference room at Burford. Edwina gave instructions for the session and gave the date and time. "This is a formal deposition to gather facts in the case of Jessie Batelle's nonrenewal by Burford College. Our court reporter will be taking down the proceedings." She nodded toward a plump woman in a gray suit who sat near one end of the table.

Al raised his eyes from the papers in front of him

and said in a bored voice, "I object to a deposition being taken from Ms. Effelton. She's not on the Burford faculty. I don't see what she has to do with this case."

Edwina, already prepared for this objection, said, "She has been on the faculty; she coached the women's golf team two years ago in the spring semester. She was also partners with Chris Stendal who was killed and who was involved with this case."

Pam tensed and said, "Killed? She committed suicide."

Edwina said, "If you're going to testify, you'll have to be sworn in. Do you promise to tell the truth, the whole truth, and nothing but the truth, so help you God?"

Pam answered, "Yes."

Rolling his eyes toward the ceiling, George said in the direction of the court reporter, "All right, but for the record, I object to this whole thing." The court reporter nodded as she typed away on her machine.

"Now, Ms. Effelton, tell us in your own words what your relationship was to the deceased, Chris Stendal," Edwina began.

"Uh, we were partners," Pam said, shifting in her chair.

"And how do you define that?"

"Well, we shared everything — our lives, you know," Pam said, choking up a little.

"I realize some of this might be difficult for you," Edwina said kindly."Was one of the things you shared a residence in faculty housing so that the college was aware of your relationship?"

"Yes," Pam answered.

"By sharing do you mean talking about friends, problems, and how things were going at work for both of you?" Edwina asked.

"Yes," Pam said.

"For how long did you 'share everything' — how long were you together?"

Al interrupted, "I object. What has this got to do with anything?"

Edwina said, "Record the objection. Answer the question, Ms. Effelton."

"We were together five years, until —" Pam's voice wavered.

"Five years. That would mean that your relationship predated Chris Stendal's taking the full-time position at Burford? So you moved to Burford together?"

Pam flushed. "Not exactly. We were having difficulties. I came just before Christmas."

"So you weren't sharing everything at that point? You were estranged?" Edwina said gently.

"It was just a misunderstanding. We had a commitment ceremony that spring hosted by faculty members. Everyone was invited." Pam shrugged.

"By everyone, do you include students?" Edwina asked.

"No, faculty and their partners and some staff," Pam said, looking relieved that the line of questioning had shifted away from her relationship with Chris. Jessie worried that Pam had been let off the hook.

"How did the college feel about students knowing about your relationship?"

"Objection, irrelevant," Al interrupted.

Edwina nodded and continued, "Answer the question."

"Nothing was said one way or the other, but it was pretty common knowledge that the students were homophobic and that bad evaluations were taken seriously," Pam replied.

"So it wouldn't be safe to be very open to students?"

"Right," Pam said.

Jessie thought, Well, at least that's acknowledged.

"What were Chris's feelings about her position at Burford when she took it? Isn't it true that she came without a Ph,D,?" Edwina asked.

"Well, she told me it was a good opportunity. Jobs were very hard to find, especially without a Ph.D. She was still working on her dissertation. She felt good because she talked them into making the position full-time."

"Would you say that she intended to stay in such a position? It was a staff position, wasn't it? Not a position for which a Ph.D. was needed?"

"No, I don't think it was her dream position; she saw it as good experience. Her degree was in Women's Studies and she would be working with women," Pam answered.

"Then she would have seen the position as Director of Women's Studies as a better career choice? Why didn't she apply when it came open?" Edwina asked.

"Yes, she wanted that position, but she was told that she wouldn't be considered because her Ph.D. was not completed," Pam said.

"Who told her she wouldn't be considered?"

Al shot a warning look at Pam, but she wasn't looking at him. "As I recall, it was Denise Oberon, who was chair of the search committee. Besides that, Chris wasn't even allowed to be on the search committee, and some of the interviews were scheduled when she was to be out of town, even though she would have to work with the person," Pam said icily.

"And how did she feel about that?"

"She was angry; she felt unappreciated." Pam shifted in her chair and glared at Edwina.

Jessie passed Edwina a note to ask about Chris's feelings about Denise as Acting Director.

Looking up from the slip of paper, Edwina asked, "Denise was also Acting Director for a year before the new director was hired, was she not?" At Pam's affirmative answer, she went on, "And how did Chris feel about that?"

"Well, she took on a lot of the director's duties herself. Denise didn't get over to the office much, even though to hear her, she did more work than all previous directors," Pam said with a sneer.

"So, how did Chris feel when the new director was hired?" Edwina asked calmly.

"She tried to like her, but it was just too much." Pam glanced at Jessie and looked away.

Edwina asked, "What do you mean?"

Pam said through clenched teeth as she glared at Jessie,"Well, if you want to know, Chris thought she was uppity. She wanted to make changes without consulting Chris. It was as if she didn't care what Chris thought or about all the things she'd had to do to try and please everyone. Who did she think she was? When you come right down to it, the job should have been hers. She was already doing it. How would you feel?" She turned her gaze to Edwina.

"Was there a point at which you remember her saying or doing something to make the job hers?"

"Objection!" Al said firmly, but unable to contain herself, Pam interrupted forcefully.

"The job should have been hers. This woman had no right to come in and take it." Pam thrust a finger at Jessie who shrank back a little in her seat. Pam continued, her face flushed. "When evaluation time came up, we talked about the letter she would write to discredit *Ms.* Batelle," she said sarcastically. "What did Chris and I owe her? Why shouldn't we write a letter that would make them favor Chris?"

"And why did she think the letter would get her the position?"

"By then she had her Ph.D. — Denise Oberon and the others couldn't tell her she wasn't eligible. And she was in pretty tight with the administration. She had made them look very good with her multicultural women's events so they'd take her seriously. She was convinced she was the best person for the job, better than the current director," Pam said hotly.

"It's true, isn't it, that she didn't get the position although the letter got my client removed, as you said?" Edwina said.

Al objected, running his hand through his carefully waved, distinguished gray hair.

Again Edwina directed her to answer the question.

"I don't know," Pam answered, tight-lipped.

"You don't know or you don't want to say?" Edwina pushed.

Pam said nothing, frowning, her face still flushed. Jessie could feel the tension in the room.

"Did it have something to do with what Georgia Swain found out and was going to make public before she was killed?" Edwina asked.

"The police said her death was an accident!" Pam snapped. "Why do you insist on calling the deaths 'killings'?"

Recovering from Pam's verbal attack, Jessie passed Edwina a note that said: "I saw Pam leaving the bike trail with a golf club right before I found Georgia. Ask Pam about Chris's relationship with Georgia." Edwina visibly brightened.

"What was Chris's relationship with Georgia Swain like?" Edwina asked.

"What relationship? She didn't have a relationship with Georgia!" Pam thundered, rising half out of her seat.

Jessie could feel Pam starting to unravel. If only Edwina could continue the momentum.

"What about Joyce Barnette? Did she have a relationship with Joyce?" Edwina asked, playing on Pam's sudden anger.

"You bitch!" Pam shouted, lunging across the table at Edwina. "Yes, she was a slut! She deserved what she got! All of them deserved it! She betrayed me. I loved her. How could she? Joyce wanted me to look like a fool. She could have Chris when I couldn't! And Georgia wouldn't keep her nose out of it! She thought she knew everything! So I had to get rid of both of them. And then Chris decided she'd just desert me after I got rid of both of them for us. And now — you interfering bitch!"

Pam was around the table with her hands on Edwina's neck when Detective Carin burst into the room. It took three of them to drag her off Edwina and subdue her.

When Pam and the detective left, Edwina, a little shaken, winked at Jessie. "The settlement is looking better and better," she said.

CHAPTER 20

Jessie and Lynn sat in the living room of the little faculty house waiting for a call from Detective Carin. The Grand Jury was deliberating on whether there was enough evidence for Pam Effelton to go to trial for the murders of Joyce Barnette, Georgia Swain and Chris Stendal. Jessie had testified that morning that she had seen Pam leaving the bike path before she found Georgia. In the ensuing time since the deposition, a search had been made of the house that Pam and Chris had shared. The police came up with the golf club believed to have been

162

used to hit Georgia in the head before she went off the bridge on her bike. They also found the same kind of copper wire used to trip Joyce. A copy of the threatening flyer that Jessie had found on her windshield had also turned up. Most damning was the confession Pam had given at the deposition. The wire and flyer could be seen as circumstantial, but the club showed traces of blood and hair which the police were confident would match Georgia's when the body was exhumed. The police had also found Pam's fingerprints on the ceiling crosspieces where she had tied the rope to hang Chris in her hood.

The phone rang and Jessie reached over to pick up the one on the table by her chair. It was Detective Carin. "How did it go after we left?" she asked.

"Just as we figured, our plan worked. She was bound over for trial for all three murders. I want to thank you for your help. Your idea about getting Pam to incriminate herself at the deposition was great. I know it must have been a little frightening to confront her when you didn't know what she'd do, especially after your experience with her in your office."

"And the other night with her dog. The cats are just recovering, as is my head," Jessie interjected.

"Well," he continued, "you certainly saved us some trouble. Anything on the settlement from the college?"

Jessie answered happily, "When we got home, there was a message on the answering machine from our lawyer that the college has agreed to pay me a year's salary in settlement. Of course, I'm not supposed to discuss the specifics with anyone, but she's sure that the intent of Chris and Pam to ruin my reputation is what changed their minds. They don't want the procedural irregularities made public. So, even though this has been an ugly experience at Burford, the settlement helps."

"Have you found out anything about Pam's motive for murdering Chris?" she asked, rubbing the calico behind her ears.

"Chris apparently accepted another position and was preparing to leave *without* Pam," he answered.

When Jessie hung up, she went over to sit with Lynn on the couch where she was sorting the mail.

"It's over," Jessie said. "I'll probably have to testify at the trial, but I don't have to fear for my life anymore, and I'm out of this hostile environment. Detective Carin thought that the fact that the flyer was found at Pam's indicated that I was also a candidate for murder, but at the time the letter had done the trick instead. It wouldn't have taken much more for Pam to want to get rid of me, though, and probably you too, when she found out that we were snooping around. They found my notebook in her house too, but they think she just didn't have time to go through it. Look what she did to Georgia. The cops think Georgia found out about her and Chris's violent relationship and was getting suspicious about Joyce Barnette's death."

Lynn was reading a brochure, hardly listening to Jessie.

"What have you got?" Jessie asked.

"I know what we should do with some of the money you're going to get from Burford," Lynn said, smiling, a note of excitement in her voice.

"You do? What?" Jessie asked, grabbing the kitten

and hugging her. She was so happy that things were finally settled. The kitten purred and then leaped from her lap.

"Look at this — Olivia Cruises. Four to ten days on a boat of all women to exotic destinations!" Lynn said.

"A cruise? Well, we only have to find me another position and move, but why not? Jessie replied, thinking that the coming year was sure to be an adventure, but it could hardly be worse than the last few at Burford. She'd be a bit more wary of believing in an ideal lesbian-feminist community in her next position. It would take a long time to get rid of the pain of the last few years, but they'd do it. Might as well live for today, she thought, instead of some mythic future. Bring on the cruise!

A few of the publications of
THE NAIAD PRESS, INC.
P.O. Box 10543 • Tallahassee, Florida 32302
Phone (904) 539-5965
Toll-Free Order Number: 1-800-533-1973
Mail orders welcome. Please include 15% postage.
Write or call for our free catalog which also features an
incredible selection of lesbian videos.

HOODED MURDER by Annette Van Dyke. 176 pp. 1st Jessie
Batelle Mystery.   ISBN 1-56280-134-1 $10.95

WILDWOOD FLOWERS by Julia Watts. 208 pp. Hilarious and
heart-warming tale of true love.   ISBN 1-56280-127-9   10.95

NEVER SAY NEVER by Linda Hill. 224 pp. Rule #1: Never get involved
with . . .   ISBN 1-56280-126-0   10.95

THE SEARCH by Melanie McAllester. 240 pp. Exciting top cop
Tenny Mendoza case.   ISBN 1-56280-150-3   10.95

THE WISH LIST by Saxon Bennett. 192 pp. Romance through
the years.   ISBN 1-56280-125-2   10.95

FIRST IMPRESSIONS by Kate Calloway. 208 pp. P.I. Cassidy
James' first case.   ISBN 1-56280-133-3   10.95

OUT OF THE NIGHT by Kris Bruyer. 192 pp. Spine-tingling
thriller.   ISBN 1-56280-120-1   10.95

NORTHERN BLUE by Tracey Richardson. 224 pp. Police recruits
Miki & Miranda — passion in the line of fire.   ISBN 1-56280-118-X   10.95

LOVE'S HARVEST by Peggy Herring. 176 pp. by the author of
Once More With Feeling.   ISBN 1-56280-117-1   10.95

THE COLOR OF WINTER by Lisa Shapiro. 208 pp. Romantic
love beyond your wildest dreams.   ISBN 1-56280-116-3   10.95

FAMILY SECRETS by Laura DeHart Young. 208 pp. Enthralling
romance and suspense.   ISBN 1-56280-119-8   10.95

INLAND PASSAGE by Jane Rule. 288 pp. Tales exploring conven-
tional & unconventional relationships.   ISBN 0-930044-56-8   10.95

DOUBLE BLUFF by Claire McNab. 208 pp. 7th Detective Carol
Ashton Mystery.   ISBN 1-56280-096-5   10.95

BAR GIRLS by Lauran Hoffman. 176 pp. See the movie, read
the book!   ISBN 1-56280-115-5   10.95

THE FIRST TIME EVER edited by Barbara Grier & Christine Cassidy. 272 pp. Love stories by Naiad Press authors.
ISBN 1-56280-086-8   14.95

MISS PETTIBONE AND MISS McGRAW by Brenda Weathers. 208 pp. A charming ghostly love story.   ISBN 1-56280-151-1   10.95

CHANGES by Jackie Calhoun. 208 pp. Involved romance and relationships.   ISBN 1-56280-083-3   10.95

FAIR PLAY by Rose Beecham. 256 pp. 3rd Amanda Valentine Mystery.   ISBN 1-56280-081-7   10.95

PAXTON COURT by Diane Salvatore. 256 pp. Erotic and wickedly funny contemporary tale about the business of learning to live together.   ISBN 1-56280-109-0   21.95

PAYBACK by Celia Cohen. 176 pp. A gripping thriller of romance, revenge and betrayal.   ISBN 1-56280-084-1   10.95

THE BEACH AFFAIR by Barbara Johnson. 224 pp. Sizzling summer romance/mystery/intrigue.   ISBN 1-56280-090-6   10.95

GETTING THERE by Robbi Sommers. 192 pp. Nobody does it like Robbi!   ISBN 1-56280-099-X   10.95

FINAL CUT by Lisa Haddock. 208 pp. 2nd Carmen Ramirez Mystery.   ISBN 1-56280-088-4   10.95

FLASHPOINT by Katherine V. Forrest. 256 pp. A Lesbian blockbuster!   ISBN 1-56280-079-5   10.95

CLAIRE OF THE MOON by Nicole Conn. Audio Book —Read by Marianne Hyatt.   ISBN 1-56280-113-9   16.95

FOR LOVE AND FOR LIFE: INTIMATE PORTRAITS OF LESBIAN COUPLES by Susan Johnson. 224 pp.
ISBN 1-56280-091-4   14.95

DEVOTION by Mindy Kaplan. 192 pp. See the movie — read the book!   ISBN 1-56280-093-0   10.95

SOMEONE TO WATCH by Jaye Maiman. 272 pp. 4th Robin Miller Mystery.   ISBN 1-56280-095-7   10.95

GREENER THAN GRASS by Jennifer Fulton. 208 pp. A young woman — a stranger in her bed.   ISBN 1-56280-092-2   10.95

TRAVELS WITH DIANA HUNTER by Regine Sands. Erotic lesbian romp. Audio Book (2 cassettes)   ISBN 1-56280-107-4   16.95

CABIN FEVER by Carol Schmidt. 256 pp. Sizzling suspense and passion.   ISBN 1-56280-089-1   10.95

THERE WILL BE NO GOODBYES by Laura DeHart Young. 192 pp. Romantic love, strength, and friendship.   ISBN 1-56280-103-1   10.95

FAULTLINE by Sheila Ortiz Taylor. 144 pp. Joyous comic lesbian novel.   ISBN 1-56280-108-2   9.95

OPEN HOUSE by Pat Welch. 176 pp. 4th Helen Black Mystery.
ISBN 1-56280-102-3   10.95

ONCE MORE WITH FEELING by Peggy J. Herring. 240 pp.
Lighthearted, loving romantic adventure.   ISBN 1-56280-089-2   10.95

FOREVER by Evelyn Kennedy. 224 pp. Passionate romance — love
overcoming all obstacles.   ISBN 1-56280-094-9   10.95

WHISPERS by Kris Bruyer. 176 pp. Romantic ghost story
ISBN 1-56280-082-5   10.95

NIGHT SONGS by Penny Mickelbury. 224 pp. 2nd Gianna Maglione
Mystery.   ISBN 1-56280-097-3   10.95

GETTING TO THE POINT by Teresa Stores. 256 pp. Classic
southern Lesbian novel.   ISBN 1-56280-100-7   10.95

PAINTED MOON by Karin Kallmaker. 224 pp. Delicious
Kallmaker romance.   ISBN 1-56280-075-2   10.95

THE MYSTERIOUS NAIAD edited by Katherine V. Forrest &
Barbara Grier. 320 pp. Love stories by Naiad Press authors.
ISBN 1-56280-074-4   14.95

DAUGHTERS OF A CORAL DAWN by Katherine V. Forrest.
240 pp. Tenth Anniversay Edition.   ISBN 1-56280-104-X   10.95

BODY GUARD by Claire McNab. 208 pp. 6th Carol Ashton
Mystery.   ISBN 1-56280-073-6   10.95

CACTUS LOVE by Lee Lynch. 192 pp. Stories by the beloved
storyteller.   ISBN 1-56280-071-X   9.95

SECOND GUESS by Rose Beecham. 216 pp. 2nd Amanda Valentine
Mystery.   ISBN 1-56280-069-8   9.95

THE SURE THING by Melissa Hartman. 208 pp. L.A. earthquake
romance.   ISBN 1-56280-078-7   9.95

A RAGE OF MAIDENS by Lauren Wright Douglas. 240 pp. 6th Caitlin
Reece Mystery.   ISBN 1-56280-068-X   10.95

TRIPLE EXPOSURE by Jackie Calhoun. 224 pp. Romantic drama
involving many characters.   ISBN 1-56280-067-1   9.95

UP, UP AND AWAY by Catherine Ennis. 192 pp. Delightful
romance.   ISBN 1-56280-065-5   9.95

PERSONAL ADS by Robbi Sommers. 176 pp. Sizzling short
stories.   ISBN 1-56280-059-0   9.95

FLASHPOINT by Katherine V. Forrest. 256 pp. Lesbian
blockbuster!   ISBN 1-56280-043-4   22.95

CROSSWORDS by Penny Sumner. 256 pp. 2nd Victoria Cross
Mystery.   ISBN 1-56280-064-7   9.95

SWEET CHERRY WINE by Carol Schmidt. 224 pp. A novel of
suspense.   ISBN 1-56280-063-9   9.95

CERTAIN SMILES by Dorothy Tell. 160 pp. Erotic short stories.
ISBN 1-56280-066-3   9.95

EDITED OUT by Lisa Haddock. 224 pp. 1st Carmen Ramirez
Mystery.   ISBN 1-56280-077-9   9.95

WEDNESDAY NIGHTS by Camarin Grae. 288 pp. Sexy
adventure.   ISBN 1-56280-060-4   10.95

SMOKEY O by Celia Cohen. 176 pp. Relationships on the
playing field.   ISBN 1-56280-057-4   9.95

KATHLEEN O'DONALD by Penny Hayes. 256 pp. Rose and
Kathleen find each other and employment in 1909 NYC.
ISBN 1-56280-070-1   9.95

STAYING HOME by Elisabeth Nonas. 256 pp. Molly and Alix
want a baby . . . or do they?   ISBN 1-56280-076-0   10.95

TRUE LOVE by Jennifer Fulton. 240 pp. Six lesbians searching
for love in all the "right" places.   ISBN 1-56280-035-3   10.95

GARDENIAS WHERE THERE ARE NONE by Molleen Zanger.
176 pp. Why is Melanie inextricably drawn to the old house?
ISBN 1-56280-056-6   9.95

KEEPING SECRETS by Penny Mickelbury. 208 pp. 1st Gianna
Maglione Mystery.   ISBN 1-56280-052-3   9.95

THE ROMANTIC NAIAD edited by Katherine V. Forrest &
Barbara Grier. 336 pp. Love stories by Naiad Press authors.
ISBN 1-56280-054-X   14.95

UNDER MY SKIN by Jaye Maiman. 336 pp. 3rd Robin Miller
Mystery.   ISBN 1-56280-049-3.   10.95

STAY TOONED by Rhonda Dicksion. 144 pp. Cartoons — 1st
collection since *Lesbian Survival Manual.*   ISBN 1-56280-045-0   9.95

CAR POOL by Karin Kallmaker. 272pp. Lesbians on wheels
and then some!   ISBN 1-56280-048-5   10.95

NOT TELLING MOTHER: STORIES FROM A LIFE by Diane
Salvatore. 176 pp. Her 3rd novel.   ISBN 1-56280-044-2   9.95

GOBLIN MARKET by Lauren Wright Douglas. 240pp. 5th Caitlin
Reece Mystery.   ISBN 1-56280-047-7   10.95

LONG GOODBYES by Nikki Baker. 256 pp. 3rd Virginia Kelly
Mystery.   ISBN 1-56280-042-6   9.95

FRIENDS AND LOVERS by Jackie Calhoun. 224 pp. Mid-
western Lesbian lives and loves.   ISBN 1-56280-041-8   10.95

THE CAT CAME BACK by Hilary Mullins. 208 pp. Highly
praised Lesbian novel.   ISBN 1-56280-040-X   9.95

BEHIND CLOSED DOORS by Robbi Sommers. 192 pp. Hot,
erotic short stories.   ISBN 1-56280-039-6   9.95

CLAIRE OF THE MOON by Nicole Conn. 192 pp. See the
movie — read the book! ISBN 1-56280-038-8 10.95

SILENT HEART by Claire McNab. 192 pp. Exotic Lesbian
romance. ISBN 1-56280-036-1 10.95

HAPPY ENDINGS by Kate Brandt. 272 pp. Intimate conversations
with Lesbian authors. ISBN 1-56280-050-7 10.95

THE SPY IN QUESTION by Amanda Kyle Williams. 256 pp.
4th Madison McGuire Mystery. ISBN 1-56280-037-X 9.95

SAVING GRACE by Jennifer Fulton. 240 pp. Adventure and
romantic entanglement. ISBN 1-56280-051-5 9.95

THE YEAR SEVEN by Molleen Zanger. 208 pp. Women surviving
in a new world. ISBN 1-56280-034-5 9.95

CURIOUS WINE by Katherine V. Forrest. 176 pp. Tenth Anniver-
sary Edition. The most popular contemporary Lesbian love story.
ISBN 1-56280-053-1 10.95
Audio Book (2 cassettes) ISBN 1-56280-105-8 16.95

CHAUTAUQUA by Catherine Ennis. 192 pp. Exciting, romantic
adventure. ISBN 1-56280-032-9 9.95

A PROPER BURIAL by Pat Welch. 192 pp. 3rd Helen Black
Mystery. ISBN 1-56280-033-7 9.95

SILVERLAKE HEAT: A Novel of Suspense by Carol Schmidt.
240 pp. Rhonda is as hot as Laney's dreams. ISBN 1-56280-031-0 9.95

LOVE, ZENA BETH by Diane Salvatore. 224 pp. The most talked
about lesbian novel of the nineties! ISBN 1-56280-030-2 10.95

A DOORYARD FULL OF FLOWERS by Isabel Miller. 160 pp.
Stories incl. 2 sequels to *Patience and Sarah.* ISBN 1-56280-029-9 9.95

MURDER BY TRADITION by Katherine V. Forrest. 288 pp. 4th
Kate Delafield Mystery. ISBN 1-56280-002-7 10.95

THE EROTIC NAIAD edited by Katherine V. Forrest & Barbara
Grier. 224 pp. Love stories by Naiad Press authors.
ISBN 1-56280-026-4 14.95

DEAD CERTAIN by Claire McNab. 224 pp. 5th Carol Ashton
Mystery. ISBN 1-56280-027-2 9.95

CRAZY FOR LOVING by Jaye Maiman. 320 pp. 2nd Robin Miller
Mystery. ISBN 1-56280-025-6 9.95

STONEHURST by Barbara Johnson. 176 pp. Passionate regency
romance. ISBN 1-56280-024-8 9.95

These are just a few of the many Naiad Press titles — we are the oldest and
largest lesbian/feminist publishing company in the world. Please request a
complete catalog. We offer personal service; we encourage and welcome
direct mail orders from individuals who have limited access to bookstores
carrying our publications.